TALES FROM THE
SCAREMASTER™

CLONE CAMP!

You don't have to read the

TALES FROM THE
SCAREMASTER™

books in order. But if you want to,
here's the right order:

Swamp Scarefest

Werewolf Weekend

Clone Camp!

Zombie Apocalypse

TALES FROM THE SCAREMASTER

CLONE CAMP!

by B. A. Frade
and Stacia Deutsch

Little, Brown and Company
New York Boston

Copyright © 2017 by Hachette Book Group, Inc.
Text written by Stacia Deutsch
Tales from the Scaremaster logo by David Coulson
TALES FROM THE SCAREMASTER and THESE SCARY STORIES WRITE THEMSELVES are trademarks of Hachette Book Group

Cover design by Christina Quintero. Cover illustration by Scott Brundage. Cover copyright © 2017 by Hachette Book Group, Inc.

Little, Brown and Company
Hachette Book Group
1290 Avenue of the Americas, New York, NY 10104
Visit us at lb-kids.com

First Edition: January 2017

Little, Brown and Company is a division of Hachette Book Group, Inc. The Little, Brown name and logo are trademarks of Hachette Book Group, Inc.

The publisher is not responsible for websites (or their content) that are not owned by the publisher.

ISBNs: 978-0-316-31727-6 (pbk.), 978-0-316-31728-3 (ebook)

Printed in the United States of America

LSC-C

10 9 8 7 6 5 4 3 2 1

Don't make the same mistake
Kaitlin and Noah made.
Don't read my book.

—The Scaremaster

I warned you.

Chapter One

"This is your fault." I was so mad it felt like my blood was on fire. I clenched my teeth and hissed, "You're always joking around, Noah." With big, clumping footsteps, I marched past him on the way to the dining hall. "Someday, someone's going to pull a prank on you, and we'll see who's laughing then!"

My hair matched my mood. It was out of control.

I tucked a stray long dark brown strand under my Camp Redwood Vines logo cap and stared back at Noah over my shoulder. We'd been told to hurry, but he wasn't even trying to keep up with me.

"Whatever," Noah muttered, shuffling his feet in the dirt.

It was only the first week of camp, and I knew that this was already his second kitchen assignment.

The first one was just one day, by himself. This time, I was being forced to come along. And it was for three whole days. A total waste of what should have been a fun weekend!

"I'm not going to apologize," Noah said, keeping his casual pace. "*You* didn't have to follow me to the boat dock. *You* didn't have to hide in the trees while I drilled those holes in that cabin's rowboat. And for sure, *you* didn't have to turn me in to the counselors!"

"*You* didn't deserve that trophy." I stopped and turned around to stare at him. Noah Silvetti was so infuriating! "You cheated."

"It's camp, Kaitlin," Noah said, finally catching up with me. "Not the Olympics." He raised one eyebrow. "Who do you think you are? Nancy Drew?" Noah laughed at his own joke, adding, "Kaitlin Wang, Girl Detective."

With a huff, I rotated on my tennis shoe heel and stomped toward the dining hall's back doors. I didn't care if he followed me or not.

I didn't deserve this.

Here's what happened:

It was very late when, through my cabin window, I saw Noah sneak out of his cabin and head toward the boathouse. I crept after him to find out what was going on, but he was far away and I couldn't see in the dark, so I gave up and went back to bed. I didn't actually figure out what he'd done until after the rowboat sunk in the middle of the lake. Noah was lucky that all the kids followed the rules and were wearing life vests, or it could have been a disaster. As it was, twelve boys struggled to swim to shore while Noah's cabin's team, laughing and pointing, crossed the finish line and claimed the trophy.

I was going to be an investigative journalist someday. And I knew that telling what I'd witnessed was the right thing to do.

So how was it possible that I was being punished too?

Director Dave said I shouldn't have been out after curfew.

Seriously? If I hadn't secretly investigated, when the cabin's boat sank, no one would have known who was responsible. I deserved a medal, not KP. Kitchen Patrol was a task given only to the worst rule breakers, and that was not me.

Director Dave actually said, "Kaitlin, I'm glad you told me what you saw, but you know better than to leave your cabin at night. Yours was a lesser crime but still a violation of camp rules." I kept replaying those words over and over in my head. "A violation of camp rules…" Did he know me at all? I was helping! I'd never intentionally violate any rules without a good reason.

For Noah, three days in the kitchen was a second-strike violation. And even though this was my first "crime," Director Dave wanted to prove a point, so here I was walking with Noah toward our joint punishment.

I opened the door to the kitchen just wide enough for me to slip through and let it slam back in Noah's face. The wire screen reverberated with a bang against the rusty hinges, barely missing his nose.

I heard Noah grunt as he pulled open the screen door for himself and stepped into the hot, sweaty room. It was a hundred degrees outside. In the kitchen, it had to be double that. A drop of sweat rolled down my forehead, and when I peeked back, I could see that Noah's dark hair was glistening with perspiration. He wore his hair so short that I could see that his forehead gleamed, and his ears, which were too big for his head, looked shiny.

I was glad I had the hat. My cheeks were flushed from the heat. I was sure I was melting.

"Welcome, Noah." A young woman greeted him first. Then me, "And Kaitlin."

"Where's Spike?" Noah asked her. The cook lowered her eyes at him as if she didn't know what Noah was talking about, so he went on, "Spike? The usual cook? Big guy. Tattoos." He rubbed a hand over his arm and across his neck to show where Spike's tattoos were located. "He made me peel potatoes on Tuesday."

The cook continued to look at him with a blank expression that revealed nothing.

I knew Spike. All the campers did. We treated him with equal parts gratitude for the food, which wasn't all that bad, and fear that we might get KP and have to work for him in the kitchen someday. Rumors were he learned to cook in prison. We'd heard that he ran the camp kitchen just like the prison one. Scary.

Looking at this new cook, I was relieved that Spike was out. If we were lucky, maybe he was gone for the whole weekend.

There was a glint in the cook's golden eyes

when she said, "There's a lot to do. I need to start preparing dinner." Her midnight-black hair was so dark it looked purple under the fluorescent lights. "You two should get started."

We were each given a pair of plastic gloves and a large white garbage bag. She pointed through a pair of swinging saloon-type doors into the dining area.

I glanced at Noah. I felt a little bad for him because he'd clearly done this before.

"When you're finished, I have other tasks for you." Her voice held an edge that gave me the chills. I wondered what "other tasks" meant and found that I'd changed my mind. I sort of wished that Spike would come back.

"Trash, trash, trash," Noah muttered as I followed him into the main room, where we ate all our meals at long tables, seated by cabin.

I surveyed the situation and moaned, "There's always so much garbage at camp."

Campers were supposed to bus their own plates after meals. But there were always things left over: napkins, wrappers, paper cups. It was like they half cleaned and left the rest, knowing, if they waited long enough, Noah would eventually be there.

I couldn't help but notice that the cook was grinning to herself, lips turned up ever so slightly at the edges, as she disappeared back through the doors into the kitchen.

We walked in silence around the edge of the mess hall, collecting paper products and leftover food. "So…" I was still mad, but staying quiet wasn't my way. "Why'd you cheat? Didn't you trust your team to win fairly?"

"I'm not talking to you," Noah retorted. "I don't know who you'll tell."

"That's not fair," I countered. "You were the one who got us both in trouble."

"You have no sense of humor," he said, voice rising. "The boat prank was hysterical!"

I grabbed two broken pencils, a frayed friend-ship bracelet, and a half-eaten sandwich from the floor. Dropping all that in my trash bag, I said, "It wasn't hysterical. It was dangerous and dumb."

Noah grabbed a paper cup off a table and tossed it at my head. "You're ruining my fun." I swerved left, and the cup missed, landing softly on the floor by my foot.

"We're even, then, because you're ruining *my* fun!" I picked it up and wadded it in a ball. "Here."

I threw the cup up and smacked it with the palm of my hand. The cup flew at him with such force and precision that it bounced off his forehead. "Ha!" I took a small curtsy. "You're looking at the captain of the middle school tennis team and twelve-year-old regional Slam Jam champion."

"La-di-da," Noah mocked. "I'm on the all-state improvisational comedy team."

"Really?" For someone who considered himself a master at being sneaky, Noah was shockingly easy to read when he was lying. "Wait. I don't believe you."

I was surprised when he answered honestly. "Well, I could have been. I was up for the team, but my parents couldn't take me to the final tryout." He went on, revealing, "They're tree huggers. Seriously, if you look up the word online, you'll find my parents hugging trees. They are always out in the woods, finding themselves, or writing books on berries, bugs, or leaves." He added in a softer voice, "I have a nanny, but she doesn't drive."

This little bit of honesty was so unlike what I knew about Noah—I didn't know how to respond.

My parents were divorced but never neglectful.

Both of them were overly committed to being at everything "for my sake." They didn't really like each other, and yet, they never missed a tennis match or a school presentation or *anything*. Noah's parents were never around while mine were always there. If they knew I had KP this week, they'd probably both come to "be with me during this difficult time." No joke.

Noah and I were finishing up, gathering the last bits of trash, when the cook popped her head out of the kitchen. Her eyes seemed golden when I'd first seen her, but now they appeared brown or blue or...I squinted. It might have been my imagination, but they kept changing.

"Dumpster's out back." She pointed toward the rear of the building. "You must stack the bags neatly inside. One of you will need to climb into the dumpster to make sure the trash is organized."

"Organized?" I heard Noah mutter under his breath. "Spike never made me organize the garbage."

The cook acted as if she hadn't heard him. "After you're done there, come find me."

If she wanted the trash organized, it would be

organized. There was no way I was getting in more trouble. I hefted my full, heavy bag and headed out. "You coming?" I asked as I passed by Noah. I was determined that if anyone had to climb into the dumpster, it would be him.

"Right behind you," he said. Then he snatched my baseball cap off my head.

"Hey." I spun around to face him. "Give that back!"

Noah took off running. The big white trash bag banged against his legs as he dashed out the dining hall door and around to the large, green metal dumpster.

Tennis requires conditioning, and Noah had no way to know that I loved running. He didn't expect it when I caught up easily and leapt forward to block the way between him and the dumpster.

I rested my trash bag on the ground, put one hand on my hip, and stretched out the other. "Give me my hat."

I worked hard to get that camp hat, and I was not giving it up. I was already twelve years old, and this was my first summer at camp. There were a lot of summer camps around the lake, but Camp Redwood Vines was the smallest. I used that fact to convince my parents to send me. I assured them it would be "safe," that the counselors would know everyone and always be around, so nothing bad could possibly happen.

"Go get it," Noah said with a laugh, tossing it up and over my head. The hat landed in the dumpster.

"You're not funny!" I grit my teeth as I realized that I was going to have to be the one to climb over the side. I hefted myself up the narrow ladder attached to the huge bin.

It wasn't as gross as I expected. Neat white trash bags were piled in low rows. The cook was right—it certainly was "organized," strange as that sounded. The trash smelled bad, but at least it wasn't leaking out all over the place.

I lowered myself into the dumpster between two full bags of something so stinky I gagged. Happiness surged through me at the sight of my hat sitting on a clean cardboard box. I grabbed it and was about to quickly call to Noah to hand over the trash bags when a bit of leather caught my eye.

"Hey, Noah. I found an old book." My voice

echoed a little off the dumpster walls. The discovery was so exciting I temporarily put aside that I was mad and that I didn't like him. I turned the book over in my hands. "It's an antique, I think... definitely not trash. There are these strange gash marks in the leather cover."

"Gash marks?" Noah climbed up the little ladder so he could peer into the dumpster. "Show me."

The strange thing about my discovery was that it didn't completely feel like a discovery—it was like the book was waiting for me. Sure, it was tucked between two white bags, but anyone who'd climbed into the dumpster would have easily found it there.

I studied the small brass locking clasp that stretched from the cover to the binding. Etched into the cover, beneath those long scratch marks, was a geometric design made entirely of the same size triangles, all in a deep golden color.

The book was so interesting on the outside, and I couldn't wait to see what was inside. Filled with anticipation, I pushed aside the clasp and opened the cover.

"Ha-ha-ha." I fake laughed as disappointment flooded over me. "Come on, Noah. Will you ever stop joking around?" It was so obvious that he threw my hat into the dumpster on purpose so I'd find the book and get set up for some elaborate Noah Silvetti prank!

"What are you talking about?" he replied, playing dumb.

"The book has your name in it." I rolled my eyes at him as I climbed out of the dumpster and pushed past him down the ladder. "Is this your way of getting back at me for reporting you? You leave a mysterious book in the trash dump; then, when I find it, you can accuse me of stealing your journal. Is that your plan? You want me to have KP for the entire summer?"

"What are you talking about, Kaitlin?" Noah repeated, staring at the book in my hands.

I leaned in and looked closely at him. I could see he was confused. Could it be that this wasn't a trick after all?

Nah. I shook the thought away. Of course it was a trick. I handed him the leather-bound journal to see what he'd do.

Noah opened the cover and read out loud:

Tales from the Scaremaster

Then below that, the story began.

Once upon a time, there was a boy named Noah....

Chapter Two

"I didn't write this," Noah told me.

"Of course you didn't," I said, putting my hands on my hips. "You never do *anything*...."

I watched Noah skim through the book's pages. They were thicker than any other journal I'd ever seen. Clean with a light tea-colored tint. Unlike the cover, which had obviously been intentionally damaged, the inside pages all looked the same, perfectly even, one identical to the next. It was weird: The outside was old and weathered, but the inside was crisp and brand-new.

Noah said, "This isn't my book. Why would I write a story about myself? There must be another Noah at camp."

"I don't know one. Do you?"

He didn't answer because we both knew that there were 150 kids at camp, and he was the only Noah.

I couldn't believe it. I'd caught him red-handed and yet he continued to pretend the book wasn't his. "Are you saying you *don't* keep a journal?"

Noah paused for a long moment. "I do," he admitted. "I mean, I have a notebook where I write down pranks and ideas for jokes and stuff. But…" He held up the leather-bound book. "Mine was a gift from my parents. It's made of recyclable paper, and if you bury it, it grows into a field of flowers."

I laughed.

"I wish I was kidding," he said with a frown.

Noah ran his hand over the journal's leather cover, tracing the long white scratches with a fingertip. "Can you imagine if this was mine? My parents would kill me and then kill me again."

I didn't know his parents but now had enough information about them to make a guess. "Because it's leather?" I asked.

"Exactly. Would you like to hear a speech on the vegan life?" He gave a wry smile. "I have it memorized. When I eat out, it has to be in places they will never find me." He rubbed his belly. "I'm a carnivorous rebel."

That made me laugh again. I was almost willing to believe the journal wasn't his. But then again, Noah had quite the secret life. Pranks and meat-eating. What else was he hiding? I put on my investigator's cap (well, the camp baseball hat) and asked him to prove the journal wasn't his.

"How am I supposed to do that?" Noah turned back to the first page. "Someone put my name right here." He pointed to the sentence.

"Exactly. So that settles it," I said. "It's yours." I narrowed my eyes. "What are you up to, Noah?"

"I'm telling you, this isn't mine." He was frustrated. "I've never seen it before."

"Don't mess with me," I warned. "I'm still mad at you." I touched the brim of my hat and stared at him.

"I know what to do," Noah said, his voice fast and a little desperate. "You like hard facts, so let me show you. This isn't my handwriting."

I still hadn't tossed my trash bag into the dump, so I grabbed it. I found one of the broken pencils I'd thrown away and passed the stub to Noah, wiping my hands on my jeans afterward. "Go ahead," I said, nodding toward the journal. "Prove it."

"Okay, I will."

There was a smooth patch of ground under a tall tree a few feet from the dumpster. Noah sat down and balanced the journal on his thigh while I tied up my trash bag and stacked it in the bin. Then I sat next to him, leaning back on the tree trunk.

In a bit of white space directly beneath *Once upon a time, there was a boy named Noah*, he scribbled:

This is Noah's handwriting.

I looked at the handwriting and at the beginning of the story above it. "I'm no expert, but that looks the same to me."

Noah leaned in closer to the words. He squinted. "It does kind of look the same. Hmmm. Must be a coincidence. My handwriting isn't usually so scratchy."

"It's not a coincidence, since the book is yours," I said, starting to rise. "We need to get back to the kitchen. So whatever joke you're playing, stop it now."

"There's no joke," Noah insisted. "Let me try again."

He wrote:

Once upon a time

And then:

This is not my book.

"My handwriting looks a little different today. Must be the book's thick paper, or your garbage pencil." He turned the page to me so I could see how he lined up his letters beneath the original sentence. "Check it out, my *o*'s look nothing like the book's *o*'s."

"You can't fool me," I said. "They're the same." I bent over his leg to get a closer look at the writing.

Noah was determined to prove the book wasn't his. He wrote:

Whose book is this?

I was comparing the *k*'s and *t*'s when suddenly words appeared underneath Noah's question.

It's my book.

I jumped back so fast I accidentally knocked the book off Noah's lap and into the dirt.

"So that's your joke?" I said, standing up and

dusting off my pants. "You have a book that writes back." I knew he was up to something! "Ha-ha-ha." I gave a sarcastic laugh. "Okay, so you had me scared for, like, a second." I stared at him with hard eyes. "Now the prank's revealed. So how'd you do that?"

Noah was staring, mouth open, eyes wide, at the book lying in the dirt. When he didn't move, I reached out to pick it up.

"No! Kaitlin, no!" He grabbed my arm and pushed me back, as if to protect me. He stood between me and the journal. "It's possessed!"

"What are you talking about?" I shoved past Noah and snatched the book. "Enough fooling around, Noah. We gotta go. I don't want to be late and get extra KP. Three days in the kitchen with you is bad enough." I held out the journal. "Take it. Try your joke on someone else."

When he didn't move, I turned to look at him. The expression on his face was one of terror. "Something is weird and wrong," he said. "This isn't a joke." Noah took a finger and crossed his heart. "I promise."

"Impossible," I said. "Books don't write themselves."

"I know…" His voice was a whisper. Moving cautiously, Noah took the book from me. He held it at arm's length, as if afraid to get too close to it. When he sat back down in the dirt, Noah motioned for me to sit with him.

He rubbed the broken pencil on a nearby rock to sharpen the tip, then, with a shaking hand, wrote:

Who are you?

The book wrote back right away:

The Scaremaster

I looked to see if Noah had pressed a button or done some kind of magic trick. If so, it wasn't obvious. And yet, I pointed at the top of the page where it said: *Tales from the Scaremaster*.

"I'm not the Scaremaster, if that's what you think," Noah said, then wrote:

What do you want?

To tell you a story.

"Uh, what if we don't want to hear one?" Noah asked me. There was a tightness in his voice. He glanced at me and said, "This is kind of creepy, don't you think?"

"This is ridiculous," I said, getting up and taking a few steps toward the dining hall. "The book isn't talking to us on its own. That's scientifically impossible. Everything can be explained," I told him. "In fact..." Something important was nagging at the back of my mind.

I looked around camp, and my brain started spinning.

Beyond the dining hall, past the infirmary, was a thick woodsy area of camp, like a small forest on a hill. In the other direction were the lake and the crafts areas. Every building at camp looked like Abraham Lincoln had designed it out of logs, and everything was named after a tree.

The lake was Walnut Lake. The crafts area was really just picnic tables and a small storage shed by the boathouse, glamorously called Pine Corner.

All the names were cheesy, but I liked them—they fit the Redwood Vines theme.

Noah and I were at the Dogwood Dining Hall. To

the left there were eight cabins, four for boys and four for girls, all labeled by colors of leaves in fall. Noah lived in Cyan. I was in Ochre. There was Umber and Magenta. Cloud and Khaki. Spice and Plum. But we all called them normal names: Blue, Yellow, Brown, Pink, White, Beige, Orange, and Purple.

More to the left were activity areas, like the gaga pit, ball fields, and the ropes course. That whole part of camp was called Oak Orchard, though it was neither oak nor an orchard. The only thing not cleverly named was the recreation center, which was the largest building at camp, and directly in front of us. The logs that formed the sides were huge. It was the called the Rec Center, or officially "the SRC"—no one knew what the *S* stood for. Last year, it was the Maple Leaf Rec Center. I knew that because they hadn't changed the sign when they changed the name.

Past all the buildings, around another small hill from the baseball field, the stables, and the maintenance shed, there was a fence. The fence separated camp from a grassy field that was rumored to have once been a cemetery. To me, it looked like any other field of grass.

It was the cemetery and the whole "hauntedness" of it that drew my attention. I was sick of camp rumors. Whether it was about Spike's time in prison, the haunted cemetery, or today's whispered warning that kids who went into the infirmary would never come back again, I firmly believed what I told Noah, "Everything can be explained."

These were stories, passed down by the counselors year after year, meant to keep campers in line.

Maybe that was what the Scaremaster's journal was meant to do as well? Scare us into behaving. It would make sense, considering Noah's reputation.

I told Noah my theory.

"You're pretty good at figuring stuff out," he said with an odd little grin. "I have to admit, I like playing pranks, not having them played on me." He turned the book around in his hands, staring at it inch by inch. "There must be some new kind of technology inside, but it looks like a regular journal to me." He tapped his fingers on the cover. "Okay. Let's read the story and find out what's going on."

Once upon a time, there was a
boy named Noah.

Noah thought camp was boring,
so he planned a few pranks to
keep himself entertained. He
didn't mind getting in trouble.
Noah was good at getting
in trouble. It was worth it,
for the fun.

But then the Scaremaster
took over.

Noah was making mischief one
trick at a time. A beginner's way.

Move over, Noah. Make room
for a professional. I'll show you
real fun. You will learn from
the master.

Prepare for double the trouble.

Two times the tricks.

It is already set in motion.

By sunset Sunday, it will
be done.

Camp will be mine. All mine
forever more.

This is the greatest prank yet.

Monday morning, the story
of what I have done here will
spread across the globe. My
name will strike terror into the
heart of anyone who hears it.

I am the Scaremaster.

Noah raised his eyes to mine.

"Is that it?" I asked.

"Yep." He shoved the text toward me.

I read the story again to myself. "Where's the rest?" I flipped page after page. They were blank.

"Kaitlin," Noah said. "I know you're still mad about everything, but we have to figure out who is behind this book. I need your help."

I barely knew the guy, but when he was lying, it was so obvious. When he was telling the truth—that was obvious too.

When he said he needed my help, I was certain Noah was telling the truth.

"Why?"

"Because it's like this book was left for us to find. I know you're curious about who put it in the dumpster. I'm curious too. And you're the best investigator I know." He quickly added, "I mean, I've *never* been caught pulling a prank before. You caught me. That tells me you're good."

"I'll think about it," I said.

"Noah! Kaitlin!" A sharp voice rang out from the kitchen door. "Where are you? You have ten seconds to get back here. I never said you could take a break. There's work to be done."

"We gotta hide the journal," Noah said. "Somewhere no one else will look."

"We? I haven't agreed to help you," I reminded him.

The cook was counting. "Ten...nine..."

"Please," he said. "Do you want me to beg?"

"No," I said. "But from here on out if I help you, you have to be truthful about everything." I added, "And no more pranks."

"Done," he said, a bit too quickly. Shouldn't he have thought about the deal a little more? Especially the "no pranks" part? He didn't even ask for how long. Did I mean the weekend? All of camp? Forever? Didn't he want to know what my terms were?

"Oh, fine." I gave in. The part of me that was curious about the book was bigger than the part that was mad. I'd be careful. If it turned out Noah was behind it, I'd figure that out fast and immediately go back to being mad at him. We shook hands.

Then I pointed to the dumpster. "No one else at camp is dumb enough to look in there. *We* will come get the book again after the kitchen closes."

"I'll climb in next time. It's my turn to stink." Not worried about the organization of the bags, Noah hefted his trash bag into the dump, then tossed the book over my head, like he'd done with my hat. It clattered into the dumpster with a satisfying bang, and then we ran.

"Two, one..."

We made it back to the kitchen just in time.

Chapter Three

Dinner KP was a disaster.

It started out okay. When Noah and I got back to the kitchen, the cook asked us if everything had gone "according to plan" at the dumpster.

"Uh, yes?" I said, more like a question than an answer. This woman was so strange! I definitely hoped Spike would be back soon.

"Very good," she said, those bizarre colored eyes twinkling, and then she repeated, "Very good," before assigning me to cut veggies for salad while Noah stacked trays and made sure there were enough napkins in the dispensers.

When the campers arrived, our task was to walk around refilling drinks and being generally helpful.

I felt lucky to have the best counselors in the whole place. Everyone said so. Samantha and

Sydney were in college. They were blond twins from the Midwest and the nicest people I'd ever met.

When we first arrived at camp, they had decorated the cabin with Welcome banners. That same afternoon, they helped us set up our beds. Then, that night, they gave us all matching flashlights with our names bedazzled on them as presents.

Their niceness made me want to be extra nice back. Since I had kitchen access, I went to my cabin's long table and asked them if they wanted seconds on anything or extra dessert.

I didn't expect what happened next.

Sydney pinned me with one green eye and shouted, "Fire!" to my entire cabin. The girls, who a minute earlier had been my friends, started throwing stuff at me. Not just napkins, but cups, bowls, plates. I even dodged a knife.

"That was a good one," Samantha said to the girl who'd nearly turned me into Vincent van Gogh. Okay, so it wasn't that close, it was plastic, and I can dodge pretty much anything, but still, it was a KNIFE!

"Try the fork," Samantha said, passing a clean one down the table to Josie Garcia, my upper bunkmate.

"Josie!" I shouted from behind one of the thick wooden pillars that held up the mess hall roof. "What are you doing? Stop!"

The fork sped toward the pillar like a four-pronged arrow, then bounced to the floor.

Noah had been in the kitchen getting extra dessert for his own cabin when the attack began. "Kaitlin!" He set the tray he was carrying on the closest table and boldly rushed through the onslaught to my side. We were near an empty table where the director usually sat. Director Dave wasn't there, so Noah tipped the table on its side and we ducked behind it like a shield.

"What is going on?" I asked him. My counselors were now encouraging other counselors to throw stuff around the dining hall. Broccoli, bits of chicken, and that salad I'd made were sticking everywhere from the floor to the rafters. I saw a tomato smash against the window, red juice and slippery seeds sliding down toward the floor.

And then the chanting began. "Clean up, Kaitlin...." It was like a loud cheer, repeated over and over again.

Noah peeked out from behind our table barricade. His counselors were taking videos on their phones. Kids weren't allowed phones at camp, but the counselors had theirs. If my parents saw this on the camp website, I'd be home faster than I could inhale a breath.

"Why are they picking on me?" I asked Noah. "I swear, if you already broke our agreement..."

"I didn't," he promised. "I don't get it." He pressed my head down behind our safe barrier as a tray soared like a Frisbee over our heads. "I'm on your team." He stood. "I'm going to stop this."

I would have expected Noah to rush out and join the fun, but instead, he marched through what was now a multi-cabin food fight, straight up to Samantha and Sydney. "Stop it," he said, hands on his hips. "This is bad and dangerous."

I nearly choked. He sounded like me! So serious and concerned.

But then Noah added, "Someone could slip on Jell-O and die!" He showed what that might look like: first sliding on Jell-O and imitating what it would be like to hit his head, and then choking and faking a heart attack. It was a grand death performance that ended with him slumping down to the mess-covered floor.

Samantha swooped back her long hair and

leaned over Noah, as if she was going to say something, but then she burped. Loud and smelly, right in his face. Her sister started laughing so hard that she fell backward off the bench.

Throughout the room, kids started burping at each other. It seemed like everyone was playing along.

Everyone, that is, except a few kids who had scattered to the farthest edge of the dining hall, away from the chaos. They were pressed up against the wall, leaning into a mural of the lake, as if it was a portal and leaning hard enough would make them disappear through.

Just as I saw them, Sydney did too. "Hey," she called out to them. I quickly counted six kids: three boys, three girls. "What's the matter?" she screeched. "Don't you want to leave a bigger mess for Kaitlin to clean up?" She moved fast, sliding on a tray across the floor to face them.

Shouts of "Clean up, Kaitlin!" intensified with more trash tossing.

The youngest kids at camp were in third grade. A shy boy from that cabin, wearing glasses and a nerdy superhero T-shirt said in a weak voice, "I don't want to get in trouble."

"There's no trouble," Sydney said. "This is fun!" She grabbed a cup off a nearby table and dumped the water on the floor. "See? Fun!" She grabbed another cup, filled with red juice, and held it out to him. "You dump this one. Spill it for Katy to clean up."

No one ever called me that. I cringed.

The boy shook his head strongly back and forth. He stuck his hands in his pockets.

"You don't want to play?" Sydney asked, her voice softening. I thought maybe she realized she was scaring him and was going to back away. Instead, she put her hand on the boy's forehead. "If you don't want to have fun at camp, you must be sick!" She eyed the other five kids, all mixed ages. There was even a girl from my cabin there against the wall.

Samantha came to join her sister.

"Do these kids look sick to you?" Sydney asked.

Samantha nodded, while the kids themselves shook their heads.

"Well then," Sydney told her sister. "They have to go where sick kids go."

"Not the infirmary!" The girl from my cabin

put her hands on her hips. "I refuse to go to the infirmary!"

Apparently I wasn't the only one who had heard that rumor about kids never coming back. I didn't believe it, but from where I stood, I could see that my cabin mate Becky clearly believed every word.

Samantha signaled one of the fifth-grade counselors. He was a big guy, much bigger than Becky, and she wasn't small. She had a round face and a tough build, yet he picked her up as if she weighed nothing and carried her out over his shoulder like a sack of potatoes. She smacked at his back and struggled against him the whole way, screaming.

After that, the other kids by the mural didn't argue. They followed another counselor, quietly and without protest, toward the nurse's office.

Six kids were gone, but what was going on with the other 142 campers and 25 counselors who all seemed to be part of the madness?

Where was the administrative staff who ran the camp? Where was the director? The cute couple who did maintenance—where were they?

Not here. And clearly, they weren't coming.

That meant that Noah and I were now the only ones not participating in the chaos. Only, no one was shouting his name....

Seeing a lull in the action, I rushed to the kitchen. Surely the cook could stop this insanity.

"Cook?" I ran through the swinging doors so fast that one swung back and hit me on the shoulder. "Oww." I sucked in the pain and shouted louder, "Cook!"

No answer.

I checked the big pantry. The walk-in freezer. I looked out the door to see if she was taking a break.

Where was she? Dinner wasn't over. She couldn't have left!

I needed one sane adult—someone, anyone—who didn't want to pelt me with carrots!

Unsure what to do, I turned my anger on the next person who stepped through those swinging kitchen doors.

NOAH!

"This has your fingerprints all over it!" I said, still able to hear the chants, which had now morphed to "Clean up, Katy."

"I didn't do anything," Noah insisted.

"You're lying!" I shouted at him over the ruckus. "I should never have trusted you."

"What are you talking about?" Noah asked. "I'm trying to help."

I picked a carrot slice out of my hair. "You broke your deal, so now I'm breaking mine. I wouldn't help you unmask the Scaremaster if you were the only other kid at camp!"

That ability to read Noah's face, which I was so proud of before, backfired. I couldn't trust my own instincts.

"This is your fault." I pointed back at the dining room. "I don't know when you talked to Samantha and Sydney and I don't know how you got the other kids to join in, but I'm positive that you are the mastermind behind this joke." I opened the kitchen door that led outside. "It's not funny, and I'm leaving!" I didn't turn around when I shouted, "You can clean up all by yourself."

I stomped out, around the building, past the dumpster, and toward the woods. Since I was in such a hurry to escape, I didn't really have a plan for where I was going, which wasn't my style.

There was a narrow path that led between the camp offices/staff lounge toward the director's cabin. I started down that path, but hearing footsteps behind me, I veered off, swerving around trees, going deeper into the woods. I had never been this far away from the center of camp, and in the dim of sunset, the trees cast long dark shadows across the ground.

A few more feet forward, and the trees opened to a small clearing where wildflowers grew next to white berries on stems and leafy green plants. I stopped. Being alone in nature calmed me down. It was quiet here, far from the dining hall and the chants. I wished I could just stay in this little meadow forever, or at least until the end of summer.

Feeling a little better, I reached out toward one of the plants, when a voice behind me shouted, "Katy, STOP!"

I swung my head around, instinctively pulling back my hand.

"Don't call me that," I told Noah. "Go away."

"I didn't do anything." He crossed a finger over his heart. "On my honor."

"Right," I said. "And I am a queen from a far-away island, posing as a normal camp kid."

"It must be true, then." He bowed low. "Your Highness."

"Cut it out, Noah." I shook my head. I was on the verge of tears. Camp was nothing like I'd expected. It hadn't even been a full week, and here I was, ready to go home. My parents would say, "We told you so." They'd say it was an experiment that failed, and they'd want to keep me close for the rest of my life.

I turned around so as not to face Noah with my reddening eyes.

I looked back at that green plant. Some of the leaves had bright red edges, and the whole plant looked shiny, as if it has just been dipped in fresh wax. I wanted to focus on something other than my own jumbled emotions. Once again, I reached out to touch—

"What the—"

Noah body-slammed me to the ground, pinning my hands beneath me.

"What part of 'stop' did you not understand?" he asked, refusing to get off me. "Listen, that's poison ivy. The leaves are pretty, but they are covered with urushiol oil, which you don't want on your skin. It'll itch and burn." He moved aside with the knowledge I wasn't going to touch it. "You'll end up in the infirmary. And I highly doubt you want to go there."

I sat up and curled into myself, as small as I could be, just in case there was something else nearby that I shouldn't touch. "How do you know about dangerous plants?" I asked, then answered it myself. "Oh, the tree huggers." I'd nearly forgotten about his parents' obsession with nature.

Noah stood. He wandered in a small circle pointing at plants. "This one has leaves that can be brewed for tea. This one causes severe allergies—in everyone." He stooped by a berry bush. The little fruit was white with a little black "eye" on a long red stem. "If you eat these berries, you'll..." Raising one eyebrow, Noah finished, "Let's just say it's a fate worse than slipping on Jell-O."

"What's worse than dead?" I asked, recalling his death performance.

Noah shuddered like it was too horrible to consider.

"No antidote?" I wondered.

"Not that I know of."

"Those plants really shouldn't be at camp," I said.

"You left camp property back at that mossy boulder," he said, pointing back at the boundary.

"Oh," I said, staring at the rock as though it was a magical portal.

Noah held out a hand. "Let me help you up, Your Highness."

I sighed. He'd just saved me from a night of rash-covered, itchy, burning skin. If he did that, then maybe he was on my side. Maybe he was telling the truth all along.

"I'm not really royal," I admitted. "Though you can still bow to me, if you want."

He smiled, bowed low, then said, "The last prank I pulled was drilling holes in the boat. I promise."

I pinched my lips together. I stared at him. I looked back at the poison ivy. And just like that, my frustration slipped away.

"So what do we do?" I asked him.

Noah stood there for a long moment. Turning back toward the camp path, he said, "We do what we were always gonna do. We clean up. Then we get the strange book from the trash. And we find out who the Scaremaster really is, because if you ask me, I think he's behind what happened in the dining hall tonight."

"The Scaremaster might be a she," I said, thinking about the cook with the shifting eyes who had now disappeared.

"True." Noah ran a hand over his hair. "All I know is that we need to find out." He clarified, "I can't do this without you, Katy."

I lowered my eyelids and gave a small grunt. "Ugh."

"Kaitlin," he immediately corrected. "I can't do this without you, *Kaitlin*."

I wasn't ready. "I can't go back there. Not with the craziness in the dining hall. I'd rather take my chances here, surrounded by poisonous plants and dangerous leafy things."

"Everything should be okay now," Noah said. "When I left the kitchen to follow you, I went by the staff lounge. Through the window I saw that some of the staff were hanging out with a few counselors. Director Dave was there." He gave me a serious look. "I swear I saw Samantha and Sydney sitting on the couch watching TV."

"You're positive?" I asked. Hope surged through me. "How could they possibly move so fast? One minute they were in the dining hall and, a few minutes later, watching TV?"

"I wondered that too, but I am one hundred percent sure," he said. "I took a long look. I saw your counselors, and mine, plus some others, taking a break." He added, "I bet they sent the campers to the cabins with CITs to shower and get ready for bed. No more food fight."

The CITs were counselors-in-training. High-school-aged campers who weren't old enough to be counselors yet but helped out.

"Okay. I'll go back," I told him. And I agreed to help. "Cleanup's going to be a nightmare, but the faster we do it, the faster we find that book and put an end to whatever this is."

Noah smiled at me. "This is going to be as simple as stealing all the toilet paper from the girls' bathroom!"

"What?" I turned toward him. "You did that?" I thought back to the panic the first night of camp.

"Oops." He gave me a small smile and hurried toward the dining hall.

We got to the dining hall and went in through the kitchen door. A second later, I knew things were not going to be as easy as we'd expected.

The cook was still missing. I felt like there should have been a rule that an adult should always be in the kitchen.

But worse, there was a lot of noise coming from the other side of those swinging doors.

"What is going on in there?" Noah asked. I slid up next to him so we could both see through the crack between the two doors. Inside the room, the scene was just as bad as when we'd left. There was no more food to throw, so now campers and counselors were slipping around in what was already on the floor, playing made-up messy games and food-fingerprinting on the walls.

In the center of the room, my counselors, Samantha and Sydney, were cheering the kids on—still chanting my name.

"They must have come back," Noah told me.

"I'm not going in there." I shook my head.

"I'm with you," Noah agreed.

We slipped out the back of the kitchen and hid by the flagpole at the center of camp until finally— hours later—the dining hall was quiet.

Chapter Four

"Lemonhead, you'll take Junkyard and Turtle to the art shack." Samantha had called a cabin meeting. We were all sitting on the floor in front of her bunk. No one had names anymore. Everyone had nicknames, and I was stuck with Katy. "The three of you will meet up with Cricket and Scar." I glanced over at Courtney and Shandra, who seemed to dislike their new names as much as I did mine. I'll admit I was starting to feel like Katy was pretty tame compared to the others. At least it was sort of related to my own name by more than the first letter.

"The paints are in glass jars, stacked neatly on a shelf." Sydney took over the meeting. She held up a hand-drawn map of the art cabinet. "Red, orange, yellow…like a happy rainbow." She chuckled. "But when you leave the shack, they'll all be brown, brown, and brown." Her laughter spread to her sister, and the two of them gave each other high fives, then laughed so hard their voices combined into one mighty giggle.

I barely heard the stone hit the window. I had to cup my ear to hear it the second time.

While Samantha and Sydney announced the names of the group that would be letting air out of all the inner tubes by the lake, I turned to find Noah's face pressed up against the dirty glass. He was behind the cabin, his face half-covered in the shadow of an all-night safety light, looking very much like a horror-movie zombie.

"Kaitlin," he mouthed, crooking a finger as if to say, "Come here."

I refused. Cleaning up the dining hall had been the grossest thing I'd ever done in my life, and I still had two more days of KP. I couldn't risk getting in any more trouble.

I totally understood that my excuse made no sense at all considering everything my *counselors* were planning for tonight's cabin activity was both after curfew and horrendous. They had a list of ways to sabotage the camp's planned programs for the following day—mixing up the art paints and deflating the inner tubes were just two items on a long list of ways to get us all in big trouble.

What was I supposed to do? After Becky was taken away in the dining hall ruckus, another girl protested that she didn't want to be part of the group assigned to steal all the helmets from the ropes course. Samantha sent her to the infirmary too!

Simply put, I was scared to get in trouble for not doing things that would get me in trouble.

Logic was no longer welcome at Camp Redwood Vines.

The next time Noah rapped on the window, I ignored him and instead listened for my name to be called. I hoped I'd get an easy task like standing guard while the others let the horses out of the stable or even better, I could stay in the cabin and make sure none of the other cabins raided us.

"Katy Wang." Samantha called my name. My heart raced. I was about to get my assignment for the night.

I looked up slowly.

"There's someone at the window," she said, instead of telling me I had to switch all the salt-shakers with sugar or something like that.

I kept a neutral expression. "I know." In this upside-down world, I wasn't sure how else to respond. Could I get in trouble for Noah causing trouble? Wait. Yes. That was how I ended up in KP in the first place.

My brain hurt. I was getting a headache.

"Don't you want to see why that kid's here?" Sydney asked. She went to the window.

"No," I said. I really didn't. Whatever it was couldn't be good.

"I'll find out." Sydney cracked the window open a little and talked to him through the slit. "He snuck out of his cabin," she reported to us all.

"Let's hear it for Noah! Job well done." Samantha stood and applauded. Everyone, except me, followed her by clapping. They were scared not to. I held back, hoping there wasn't a not-clapping punishment.

"He wants Katy to sneak out with him," Sydney said. "Something about a book." She stepped back. "You should talk to him, Katy Lady." And there it was, my nickname was morphing into something worse. I shuddered at the thought of where it might end up.

I turned toward Noah. What was he doing here?

When we went back to the dumpster, after scrubbing every last lettuce leaf off the dining room walls, it was so late that the dump had been emptied. The book was gone.

Tales of the Scaremaster was off to some massive trash landfill in some other part of the state. No more investigation necessary. That was the end of the Scaremaster's story. Once I was done with KP, I'd be free to enjoy camp, like every other camper. That's all I ever wanted.

And yet...I glanced over my shoulder at my cabin mates—by the expressions on their faces, they didn't seem to be enjoying camp at all. They all looked like they were being forced to do things they didn't want to do.

I stepped over to the window. It was too high to climb out of but low enough that I could see Noah from the neck up. "This is a bad time," I told him. "I'll see you in the kitchen tomorrow morning." Maybe the cook would come back too? We hadn't seen her at all after dinner was served. From what I knew, KP didn't normally include preparing the entire meal. Plus, I wanted to ask her a few questions about the book. Maybe she knew the Scaremaster or something about his book.

"Look." Noah held up the leather-bound Scaremaster's journal. I could see the scratch marks in the cover, so I knew it was real.

"Where—?" I started.

"In my trunk," he blurted out. "My counselors were preparing us to raid your cabin tonight. You had such a hard day already, I decided to write a note warning you."

I had to admit, that was nice of him. Not that it would make a difference on how badly the night was turning out, but still it was nice.

Noah held the book high in the moonlight. "When I opened my trunk for paper and a pen, this was in it." I couldn't tell by his expression if he was more scared or shocked that the book had mysteriously returned to him.

The opening in the window wasn't very big, so he leaned forward to stick his face as close to mine as he could. "The trunk was locked, Kaitlin. I'm not kidding." I decided his expression was a mix of shock and fear because I was having both those feelings too.

He held the book at arm's length, by the tips of his fingers, as if it might be dangerous.

That headache I had grew stronger. The book came back? How was that possible?

Noah said, "There's more." He moved into the dim glow of the security light and cautiously opened the first page. The story we'd seen was gone. There was new writing on the page.

"Can you read it to me?" I asked. My brain was so messy inside. It felt like it was about to explode.

" 'You can't get rid of me that easily. My story is just beginning.' "

This was a lot to process. If I gave in to this headache, I'd be joining the others in the infirmary. I fought the feeling and held it together. "Is that all?" I asked.

"Sort of." Noah closed the book and reported, "Under 'Tales of the Scaremaster,' there's one more line. It's a title: 'Doubles Causing Troubles.' "

"What does that mean?" I asked.

"The original story said something about doubles too," Noah reminded me, and a little light pierced through the darkness in my head.

" 'Prepare for double the trouble. Two times the tricks.' " I closed my eyes and recited the Scaremaster's warning from memory.

The investigation was back on. I needed to

think clearly if we were going to figure out who the Scaremaster was and what the story meant. I pressed my fingers over my eyes and rubbed my temples with my thumbs, giving my brain a minute to heal itself.

"You should go with him."

I jumped back, only to discover that Samantha was now by my side. Her hair was messy and hung across her face, hiding her eyes.

"Yes, go. Sneak out." Sydney, looking very much the same, stood with her.

"Huh?" This was confusing. Counselors weren't supposed to encourage campers to sneak out in the night. Then again, they also weren't supposed to send their kids around camp destroying the next day's scheduled activities either.

Samantha shoved the small window open as far as the glass could go. I wanted to tell her that the whole reason these windows were like this was so no one could get out or in through them.

Sydney got down on her hands and knees, forming a step stool. "Stand on my back," she told me. "Then pull yourself up."

It was a weird offer, but I was scared to refuse.

More nervous than I'd ever been before, I stood on my counselor and leaned out through the window.

Then, just when I thought things couldn't possibly get stranger, they did! My counselors started working together to shove me out of the cabin.

"Maybe I should go through the door?" I asked as my belly scraped over the windowsill. "Ouch." It wasn't like I was sneaking out, so why couldn't I just walk out the door like a normal person?

"What fun is that?" Sydney said. "Doors are boring. A window escape is awesome!" My hips were stuck half in and half out of the cabin.

"Stay out all night." Samantha had a wild, sinister look in her eyes as she gave me a big push through the window. The frame splintered, and I fell to the ground at Noah's feet. Bits of wooden windowsill rained down beside me.

"No more dull Camp Redwood Vines!" Samantha said while she and Sydney high-fived on their side of the window. I noticed they had the same look in their eyes. Was it because they were twins? Or something more?

"The twins are taking over!" Sydney said. They high-fived again.

I was overwhelmed with the feeling that counselors were on the villain side of the universe, rather than the superhero.

"You okay?" Noah asked, giving me a hand up for the second time that day.

I dusted off my jeans and checked for scratches on my belly and hips. "I'm fine." I glanced back at my counselors, who were waving enthusiastically at us through the window.

"Have fun," Samantha called out.

"Fun, fun," Sydney echoed.

"Let's get out of here," Noah said, taking my hand and pulling me away.

I couldn't agree more. My headache was gone now that I was out of that cabin. I was still confused, but I felt like I could at least think clearly.

"We need to do a close examination of that journal," I told Noah as we headed toward the camp activity area. I wanted to avoid the art shed, in case my cabin mates were on their way to mix up the paints.

We ducked and dodged around Noah's cabin, then crossed the path toward the ropes course.

It wasn't quiet at camp like it should have been.

Looking back over my shoulder, I could clearly see the counselors from Cabin Khaki supervising while their campers ran someone's underwear up the flagpole. Loud voices were coming from Cabin Cloud. I cupped my ear to hear the counselors ordering the kids to put pinecones in Cabin Plum's sleeping bags. I wondered what other pranks the counselors had planned for the night. It was like the entire camp was possessed: Counselors were ordering kids to do pranks that they didn't want to do. What was going on?

"Look, Kaitlin." Noah pointed out a lone figure in the distance.

"Is that Director Dave?" I asked even though there was no way it was anyone else. He was young, tall, athletic, and totally bald. His head reflected the moonlight.

"Yeah," Noah said in a distracted whisper.

"Is he *in* the cemetery?" I squinted in the darkness.

"Yeah," Noah repeated, then fell silent.

"Shouldn't he be over here, stopping the madness?" I stopped and turned to Noah. "What are you thinking?" There was clearly something up.

"I—" His voice cut out. "It's too crazy."

I snorted. "Noah, everything that has happened today has been crazy. Spill it."

"I swear I saw the director headed to the other side of camp when I came to find you. He was walking away from the cabins, toward the infirmary, not toward the cemetery. In fact, I changed my path and hid for a few minutes behind a tree so I wouldn't bump into him." He added in a puzzled whisper, "How did he get over here so fast?"

"It's not a big deal. He changed plans." I shrugged. "He probably heard about the raids and the stuff the counselors are planning and has been wandering around to check things out." Of course, that didn't exactly explain why he'd be in the cemetery, but maybe he was checking that out too. It was possible.

"Right," Noah said after a long deep breath. "You're right. There's no way the guy could be in two places at once."

"No way," I echoed.

We walked in silence a few minutes to a picnic table at the base of the rock wall, which was part of the ropes course. It was out of the director's view. "Let's get started," I said. "Do you have a pencil?"

He still had the stub we'd saved from the trash. Placing the book on the wooden tabletop, Noah said, "I'm convinced the Scaremaster is behind everything that happened today. In that other story, he called me a beginner and him the master." Noah nearly choked on that last part. "He's trying to outprank me by pulling pranks on you."

"Well, that's a good reason to find out who it is, fast." Reviewing the day, it made sense. "Let's end the competition. I don't want to be in the middle anymore."

We needed to figure out how the book worked. Whoever the Scaremaster was also had access to the newest technology. There were a lot of campers who were into robotics. I didn't know about the counselors, but it was a place to start.

"Go on. Think like a journalist. Ask it a direct question. The more direct the better."

Noah didn't hesitate.

Did you start the food fight?

Yes.

"That was a little too easy," I remarked, biting my bottom lip.

And the raids tonight?

Yes.

I lifted the book to look underneath. "I don't get it," I muttered, more to myself than to Noah. "Where's the computer chip? Where's the On switch? Is it wireless?"

"Let me ask something that's not a yes or no," Noah suggested. "Maybe the programming is limited." He wrote:

Why are you doing this?

That was a big question. There could be a lot of possible answers. We waited for the reply.

Summer is supposed to be fun, not boring.

Okay, that was a start. We needed to find someone who was bored. That could be anyone!

Samantha and Sydney had been talking about making camp more fun. I couldn't imagine they were behind the book, but still, I tucked the possibility away in the back of my mind.

I struggled to think of something to write back that would reveal more clues. I needed to change the subject and ask something that might give us a hint to go on. Like "Where are you?" Or "How old are you?" But before I could the book started writing itself.

From now on, Noah can do anything he wants and never get in trouble. Kaitlin doesn't have to be so good about following the rules. She can lighten up.

Isn't it wonderful?

"No. I don't want to lighten up," I said, as if he could hear me. "I like me the way I am." Holding out my hand, I asked Noah for the pencil. "Can I write back?"

I was feeling personally attacked when I wrote:

I am not having fun. You're ruining
my summer.

I wondered if I should have added a question or something because the space under what I wrote stayed blank for a while. Then the Scaremaster replied:

Noah thinks it's fun. He understands a good joke.

Noah took the pencil from me and replied in big block letters:

YOUR PRANKS ARE NOT FUN.

Adding under that:

NOT FUNNY EITHER.

Noah slammed the pencil down on the table. "There," he said. "Noah Silvetti out." He gave me a grin. "I've got your back. I won't let some silly Scaremaster mess with my friends!"

Friends? Were we friends?

"I don't think writing in the journal is helping us figure out who the Scaremaster is," I said. Things had taken an unexpected turn. If the journal was run by a computer program, then all we'd discovered was that the list of responses it could make was endless.

A computer didn't make sense. But I couldn't think of anything else. I told Noah, "I think something bad is going to happen."

Then came the Scaremaster's eerie reply to confirm my fears:

I thought we would have fun together. Too bad. Plans change.

Have it your way. No more fun for you means all the fun for me!

All the writing on the page disappeared. The title "Doubles Causing Troubles" was replaced with something new. The story was now called "Twice the Terror."

And under that, words began to appear:

Once upon a time, there was a
boy named Noah

That was the same as the first time we'd opened the book, only now we were seeing the story being written. The sentence went on, adding:

and a girl named Kaitlin. . . .

I didn't want to see more. I found that any curiosity I had about who was behind the story was turning to annoyance. This guy, or girl, was like a bully poking us with a stick. The more attention we gave him, the worse things got.

"Maybe if we stop reacting to the Scaremaster, he'll just go away," I said, slamming the cover shut. I just wanted it all to end.

This animatronic book and whoever was behind it were simply making me mad.

"You mean, ignore him and he'll give up?" Noah considered that.

"Exactly," I said. "That's what my parents would tell me to do. We'll simply walk away, leave him here, and forget this all happened."

"Kids at the camp I went to last year tried that with me," Noah said. "They tried to ignore the pranks I was pulling. It didn't work. I saw it as a challenge and upped my game." He gave me a mischievous smile. "That's the reason I'm at a different camp this year. I wasn't invited back there."

While I appreciated Noah's insight, I said, "Do you have any other ideas? No offense, but I wish we could send the Scaremaster to another camp."

"I'm with you," Noah said. "There's an opening for a prankster at Camp Edwards on the other side of the lake." He gave a small laugh. "But, fair warning, they don't have much of a sense of humor over there."

We sat for a while staring at each other. A cricket chirped as the moon rose higher in the sky.

"This must be what the camp counselors felt like at my old camp, when they were trying to stop me from causing trouble. I'll admit, I don't like being on the responsible side. I don't know what to do." Noah gave up. "Let's try it your way."

"When the book was in the trash, the Scaremaster saved it before the dump truck came," I said. "We need a much better way to get rid of it for good."

Our first thought was to bury it in the cemetery. Whether it was actually a burial ground or not, everyone stayed away. It would be safe there. But then Noah reminded me that was where he'd seen Director Dave. Just in case he was still hanging around, we needed to avoid the cemetery.

We went back to the clearing where I'd nearly been poisoned by ivy. It was the opposite direction from the cemetery. Noah had a flashlight and led the way. No one ever went back there. It was off camp property, plus...those plants! They were all so dangerous, they'd act as a shield to keep people away. I doubted anyone else at camp knew as much about how to get safely around plants as Noah did.

After making sure no one had followed us, we found a hollowed-out tree, and Noah stuck the book deep inside the hole. We felt satisfied that it would stay there till the pages rotted and fell out. The Scaremaster and his journal were gone forever.

As we walked back to our cabins, Noah bragged, "Ha! Now I'm the only prank puller at Camp Redwood Vines."

Chapter Five

The next morning, the entire camp seemed exhausted from pulling pranks and staying out all night.

No one threw food at breakfast.

Samantha and Sydney were calm and didn't high-five each other during the flagpole meet-up and announcements. In fact, I wondered if Director Dave had said something to them. They were very mellow, standing at attention as the flag rose and singing the camp anthem with unusual respect. That sinister look in their eyes had been replaced by a blank stare.

Maybe they got busted for their overnight pranks? Or maybe they were just tired from so much "fun." Either way, I felt positive that, with the Scaremaster gone, today would be a great day.

Even though I'd have liked to ask the black-haired cook a few questions, I was relieved to see

Spike in the kitchen when I walked in for my first scheduled activity of the day—lunch KP. Which would be immediately followed by my second activity—dinner KP. It felt more "normal."

I mentioned the other cook to Spike and asked if he'd had a nice day off.

"No other cooks at camp," he said. He had that blank look in his eyes, similar to the one I'd seen in Samantha's and Sydney's expressions that morning. With them, it was odd and out of place. With Spike, it was terrifying, like he might snap at any second.

I didn't want to get on his bad side, so I made sure not to sound like I was arguing. "You weren't here yesterday. There was another cook and a food fight. Did you hear about it?"

"No other cooks at camp," Spike repeated more firmly than before. He was obviously a man of few words, and by his tone I understood that my question-and-answer session was over after just the two questions. He wasn't going to even discuss the food fight, so I had no way to know if he knew about it at all.

"French fries for lunch. Wash hands. Peel potatoes." He tipped his tattooed neck toward a long table. On the floor were several big burlap bags filled with brown potatoes. There were so many!

With a sigh, I washed up, then grabbed a peeler and set to work swiping off the brown skin to reveal the white flesh underneath. A few minutes later, Noah rushed through the door.

Spike turned his blank eyes toward the potatoes. Noah nodded and got to work.

"Hey," I greeted him, finishing my first potato and moving to a second.

"Sorry I'm late," Noah said. "My counselors are acting strange."

That worried me. "Strange how?"

"Normal," Noah said in a low voice so Spike wouldn't overhear us. "Too normal."

I didn't have to ask what he meant. If his counselors Jayesh and Michael were anything like Samantha and Sydney, I got it.

"It's kind of nice," I said. "Right?"

"If you like cardboard counselors," Noah said. "I even switched Jayesh's toothpaste with shaving cream this morning to see what would happen. I was late because it took him so long to get ready."

"And?"

"He brushed his teeth with it like nothing was

wrong." Noah frowned. "My senses are tingling. Something's up."

"Maybe he's ignoring you," I suggested. "Like we're doing with the Scaremaster."

"No way," Noah said. "I haven't caused enough trouble for that yet."

"Other option: I think the counselors all got busted yesterday," I told him. "They're on their best behavior today." Then I glanced at Spike, adding what I thought was more important to discuss, "He doesn't know anything about the other cook."

"Is he supposed to?" Without waiting for my answer, Noah rushed off to wash his hands. When he returned, he tossed his first peeled potato into a big silver bowl with mine and said, "If he had the day off, he might not know who replaced him."

"Sure, except he is acting like he was here." I finished another potato. Three down, a zillion to go.

"I don't—" Noah began, when Spike called out from near the stove, "No chatter. Peel potatoes!"

Noah and I took a quick glance at each other, then fell silent.

The only sound in the kitchen was the *swipe-swipe* of peelers against potatoes and the sizzle of the griddle as Spike set frozen hamburgers onto the hot stovetop. Lunch preparation went on for a while like that, until the door to the kitchen opened and Director Dave entered.

There was a mud smudge across his bald head, and he was wearing the same clothing as when we'd seen him in the cemetery. I hadn't thought anything of his white T-shirt and khaki shorts then, but now they seemed wrinkled and ragged. It wasn't just the clothes either—the director himself seemed wrinkled and ragged.

He stared straight ahead, not saying anything to me and Noah as he passed. In his hand was a note. "Work assignments are being made today for the campers," Director Dave told Spike, his voice flat. "Here's a list of the kids who will be doing KP." He waited while Spike surveyed the paper. I could see it was a pretty long list of names. "Have them do dishes or peel potatoes," he said, seeming not to realize that potato peeling was already covered.

Then the director swiveled on his heel and walked out of the kitchen, brushing so close to Noah that they nearly touched. He didn't react as he opened the screen door and stepped outside, letting it slam behind him.

"That was weird," I said to Noah.

"Shhh…" Spike gave me a warning look. I got the chills. I was feeling like that prison reputation might actually be true.

Noah scooted his foot over toward mine under the table. He tapped his tennis shoe on top of mine, as if to say, "Yeah. It was weird." And then another tap for "What is going on?"

It wasn't long before we started to see that the day was anything but normal. Jayesh, Noah's counselor who'd brushed his teeth with shaving cream, escorted ten kids into the kitchen. It was a mixed group of boys and girls, of all cabin ages. The thing they all had in common was the look of terror on their faces.

We waited, still peeling those stupid potatoes, until one of the kids got close enough to talk to.

"What's going on out there?" Noah mouthed then. He tipped his head toward the kitchen door.

"I—" The boy, who was probably in fifth grade, looked over his shoulder at Spike and fell silent.

He wasn't talking. Noah tried to get answers from two other kids before he found an older girl. I recognized her as a CIT who was *slightly* less scared than the others.

"Hey, Spike, bathroom break?" Noah called out across the kitchen. He elbowed the girl in the ribs.

"Yeah, me too?" she asked, then elbowed Noah back.

"Five minutes," Spike told them, concentrating on toasting hamburger buns. "Not six," he warned.

"Got it," Noah said, and the two of them left the kitchen.

Four minutes and fifty-seven seconds later, they came back.

"I was getting nervous," I said, dropping a potato on the floor and getting down on my hands and knees by Noah's feet to retrieve it. I didn't want Spike to hear us talking.

Noah dropped a potato too and bent down next to me.

"Victoria says all the campers have to work today." He made little quotation marks with his fingers around the word "work." Victoria was the CIT's name.

"Not activities?" I asked. I was talking very fast. We had about one more second before we had to stand up. Spike hadn't noticed us yet, but he would soon.

"Work," Noah said again. "Some cabins are going out to clear brush from that old cemetery. Other kids will be moving rocks around camp. Some will be hauling lumber from a delivery truck. Others are unloading heavy boxes that arrived this morning."

"I don't understand," I said. "What about painting with only brown paint, or finding out there are no helmets at the rock wall?"

"Canceled," Noah said. "Everything fun was canceled."

I shook my head. That headache from last night came back in an instant. I glanced across the kitchen, where Victoria was now opening cans of tuna for a massive vat of tuna salad. She didn't look my way.

"There's more," Noah said. "There are rumors

from the infirmary. Like yesterday, anyone who doesn't want to work, or complains, is being sent there. Only now the windows are blacked out and the doors are locked. No one knows what's happening inside."

"What are we going to do?" I asked, feeling panic build. We had to do something.

"We're just kids," Noah said. "What can we do?" He saw the look of horror in my eyes. "Just kidding," he said. "Joke." Noah grabbed the potato I'd dropped and handed it to me, then picked up his own. "We'll figure this out."

Chapter Six

Saturday night, after KP, I went back to my cabin, where things were on lockdown. There were no evening activities, no counselor- or camper-planned raids, because no one was allowed outside. The window I had snuck out of the night before was sealed with thick metal bars forming an X over the glass. There was no way any kid was leaving the cabin that way again.

There was no way anyone was leaving the cabin at all. Once we were inside, Samantha and Sydney moved their bunk bed in front of the door.

"What if we have to pee?" Josie, aka Junkyard, asked. The bathrooms were in another cabin central to all the girls' bunkhouses.

"Hold it," Samantha said.

"Till morning," Sydney finished.

The twins got into their sleeping bags, even

though it was only eight o'clock. Samantha on the top bunk, Sydney on the bottom.

"Lights out!" I couldn't tell which one of them said it because all the shades were drawn and the lights immediately went out.

I wasn't ready, so I turned on my flashlight.

"Lights out, Katy," one twin counselor said. Her voice was even more harsh than usual.

The other twin laughed, her voice echoing through the cabin.

I flicked off the flashlight, glad they couldn't see the annoyed expression on my face.

Luckily, it was still kind of twilight, and even with the bars on all the windows, I could see pretty well. I quickly changed into my pj's and climbed into my sleeping bag. I'd have liked to go to the bathroom to wash my face and brush my teeth, but I wasn't dumb enough to ask. I knew what the answer would be.

My cabin mates were clearly exhausted. Most of them had been assigned to moving heavy boxes into an old storage shed by the maintenance office. It meant carrying them one by one down a long, bumpy road.

I heard that their task tomorrow was going to be moving those same boxes back up the hill to the SRC, now that the fifth graders had cleared the space, putting anything that might be used for usual camp activities in storage. While there were rumors all around camp about the poor kids in the infirmary, no one had any guesses about what was in those boxes, or why Noah's junior high cabin and the fourth graders were assigned to mow down the wild cemetery grass. The CITs stacked wooden planks along the fence.

As the sound of soft snores resonated through the cabin, I felt lucky I had KP. I wasn't nearly as exhausted as the others.

Then again, it was early and I was wide awake. My worry and dread grew heavier as the hours passed.

In the morning, the counselors woke everyone up earlier than usual.

An announcement over the camp loudspeakers called out: *"All campers to the SRC!"*

"I don't think it means us," Noah said after letting me know that his night had been pretty much the same as mine. "Spike expects us early today." Noah imitated our boss, using a deep, gruff voice. "Breakfast KP. Come before campers."

"He does love short sentences," I said, focusing on that hopeful feeling that today things would be different than yesterday—or the day before.

Getting to the dining room was like swimming upstream. The counselors were dividing the kids into rows of three across, herding them from cabins to the SRC. Usually they'd have breakfast, then flagpole for announcements, but today everyone was going directly to the SRC.

The counselors walked alongside the sleepy campers, keeping them together so that no one went out of line. They must have been up late. Every counselor I saw had a glazed-over expression.

Noah and I had to walk off the path to keep from getting plowed down. No kid was brave enough to break ranks, especially not when passing the infirmary, which now had a big No Trespassing sign on it, next to one that said "Keep Out."

"It should say, 'By Invitation Only,'" Noah

said as a joke. "Get it? The counselors are choosing kids to go there—sort of like an exclusive invitation to a nightmare?"

When I didn't laugh, he said, "I think I'm losing my edge."

"Some things just aren't funny," I told him. There was nothing funny going on at camp. Crazy, maybe. Weird. Scary. Odd. Bizarre. I had a million adjectives to describe it. None of them were "funny."

One of the counselors stopped us. It was Thomas, the archery specialist. "You're going the wrong way," he said in a rough, monotone voice.

"We have KP," Noah told him.

"We were told all campers must go to the SRC, no exceptions." I didn't understand why he was talking to us that way. Thomas was usually so friendly. I stunk at archery, and he was the one who encouraged me to keep trying.

"You could ask Director Dave," I said, a rise of fear in my belly. What if he didn't let us go to the kitchen? What would Spike do? It was the last day of my punishment, I just wanted to get it over with. "Director Dave's the one who gave us this assignment."

Thomas accepted that. "Well, if he said so, go. But come back to the SRC as soon as possible."

Noah and I nodded, then quickened our footsteps on the chance he might change his mind.

When we entered the kitchen, Spike gave us a surprised look. "You aren't supposed to be here," he said in a way that made my stomach roll over. His voice was flat, just like the counselor Thomas. On Spike, it seemed so strange and got even stranger when we didn't leave fast enough. He kept that flat voice but raised it, declaring loudly, "Go! See the movie."

"What movie?" I asked, looking between him and Noah.

"For the campers," Spike said, pointing at the door with the large butcher's knife he was using. "Get out of my kitchen!" He waved the knife.

We ran, as fast as we could, out the back door and back around the building toward where the flagpole stood. We stopped in the open area. It felt so odd that no one was around.

I was breathing heavily from the mad dash, but all that tennis practice saved me. Noah was doubled over, leaning his hands on his knees. He was breathing in huge gasps of air.

"I'm too out of shape to be chased by knife-wielding kitchen prison ninjas," he said. Seeing as that was very close to the truth of what happened, I wasn't sure if that was his attempt at another joke or not.

I didn't smile. "I guess we should go to the SRC," I said, though that was NOT what I wanted to do. I had a very bad feeling about all this.

We walked side by side toward the recreation center, observing the strange silence of a camp that hosted a hundred-fifty campers, plus counselors, specialists, maintenance, staff, and a director. Why was it so eerily, unnaturally, bone-chillingly quiet?

The SRC was so large that everyone at camp could fit inside, as long as kids sat on the floor. There was a stage area for talent shows and a wide space to play in if it was raining. Basically, anything at camp could be done in the SRC if necessary. There was a big closet at the back for tables, props, whatever. The closet had a small window to the outside, from the old days when it used to be the director's office, before a special cabin was built.

We tried to look in through that window to see what was going on, but the closet door was closed.

There were other windows all around the sides of the SRC, but they were covered with the same black paper as the infirmary windows. We were going to have to take our chances at the main entry.

Very quietly, Noah cracked open the heavy wood door.

Kids were still finding seats on the floor, anxious for the program to begin. I could see that they were grouped by cabin. Mine was in the middle, to the left of the stage.

Looking past Noah, I spotted a projector and a movie screen at the front on the stage. It made me wonder if maybe there was rain in the forecast. That was when movies were usually shown.

"Come on." Noah started to go inside.

"No, wait." I pulled his arm back sharply. That bad feeling inside me exploded. We had to get away! This was wrong. All wrong. I accidentally scraped him with my fingernails as I yanked more forcefully.

"Ouch!"

"Sorry…Shhhh…" I tugged Noah back and away from the building. The door fell closed with a quiet click.

I saw movement behind one of those blacked-out windows; the shade moved slightly. Instinctively, I dropped to my knees, dragging Noah down with me, so we were under the window and out of sight. Then I started to crawl on my hands and knees as if that would keep us from being seen. Noah followed me, though I was sure he thought I'd lost my mind.

I moved us away from the SRC and didn't stop until my hands and knees hurt too bad to keep going. Then I lay on my belly in the dirt behind a medium-sized rock that provided very little cover. Noah squished in behind the rock, next to me.

"Last night, while I stared at the ceiling, I started to think. I'm pretty sure this isn't some grand prank by some random person at camp." It had been a long night, and as I tossed and turned, I came up with a theory. "I'm thinking something called the Scaremaster really exists," I said. "He's like a puppet master. And we all are his puppets."

"Kaitlin? Has an alien snatched your body? You aren't sounding like yourself." Noah pressed the back of his hand against my forehead as if I might have a fever. "I think you might be sick."

"I'm not sick." And if I was, there was no way I'd go to the infirmary. "You wanted me to investigate, and I'm telling you what I discovered." I closed my eyes and said out loud what I believed to be true. I'd realized it when we were standing at the SRC door, looking at the kids gathered on the floor. It was like I'd been hit by lightning that told me to go with my gut.

"We have to ask the Scaremaster to stop," I said, checking around that no one was watching, then crouching, and checking again before finally standing up. I started down the path toward the clearing where we'd left the book in the tree. I felt such a sense of urgency, I'd have started running if I thought Noah could keep up. Instead, I walked fast. Even then, he struggled to stay with me.

"What are you thinking?" Noah asked, his breath getting heavier with every step. "It's a supernatural book? Possessed? Haunted?"

I didn't know, so I didn't answer. Instead, I said, "Something like that. The Scaremaster has the power to make terrible things happen at camp. *Anything* he wants. He simply tells the story, and it happens." It went even deeper than that. "We don't even have to read the story. Remember how I slammed it shut after I read 'Once upon a time'— the story happened anyway." There was a part of me that wished I'd read it; then I'd know what was going on and maybe have a better idea how to stop it.

I didn't give Noah a chance to argue or try to convince me I was wrong. I rushed off the path, asking Noah to point out the bad plants so I wouldn't accidentally make a mistake and swell up like a balloon.

When we reached the tree, Noah stepped forward. "I'll get the book." He reached in and pulled out the journal. The cover was dirty and damp. There was a wafting smell of fresh paper pulp and glue. It reminded me of an antique printing press I'd once seen in a museum near my aunt's office.

"Is that the same one?" I asked Noah.

He gave me an "Are you crazy?" look. "It's a leather journal, stuck in the same tree where we left it," he said.

"It looks different," I told him.

"It's the same," Noah told me, but even so, he ran his hand over the cover where the deep scratches used to be. "It healed itself."

Now I gave him an "I told you so" look.

"Kaitlin," Noah began as we settled down on a flat rock and he was finally able to catch his breath, "you're the most logical person I know. Think about it. There's no way this book is doing what you think it's doing. There's a person behind it. Someone we know. We simply need to find out who."

I didn't defend my thinking. I couldn't have if I wanted to. "Can I take a look?"

Noah handed me the book.

I turned to the first page, where the title to this story was still written.

Twice the Terror

And under that:

> Once upon a time, there was
> a boy named Noah and a girl
> named Kaitlin. . . .

That was where I'd slammed the book shut and declared we ignore the Scaremaster.

I read on:

They didn't prepare for double the trouble. Two times the tricks. And now it's too late.

That was all that was on the page. The Scaremaster was toying with us. This was his way of saying that he wouldn't give us a second chance to read the story. The horrible nightmare he planned was happening, and there was nothing Noah and I could do to stop him.

"It's too late," I whispered on a long sigh. "It took me too long to figure this out," I muttered. "The clues were there all along."

"What are you talking about?" Noah asked, but I wasn't really listening.

"Ohhh," I moaned to myself. "What kind of investigative journalist am I? I'll have to be something else when I grow up." I was muttering. "The Scaremaster says it's too late."

"Kaitlin, what is your problem? Hand over that book." When I didn't hold it out, he took it from me. After turning to a clean page, Noah dug my pencil stub out of his pants pocket.

I nearly asked if he was wearing the same shorts for the third day in a row, but figured I didn't want to know the answer. Plus, I had more important things on my mind.

Noah wrote in thick letters:

Who are you?

The Scaremaster

Are you a camper?

No.

A counselor?

No.

Do you work at camp?

No.

"See? It's not a person at camp because *it's not a person* at all," I told Noah. Then, in a voice so low he had to lean in to hear me, I said, "I'm scared."

Noah tapped the pencil to his lips, then wrote:

Whatever you are planning, stop it now.

The Scaremaster replied:

No.

Looking at me, Noah said, "This book is broken. I think it's stuck on 'No.'" Out of frustration, he tossed the book to the side, where it landed near some of that poison ivy. Oddly, the pages seemed to pull back, curling into the cover.

"It's not a computer," I told him. I had never been so sure of anything in my life. I reached out for the book.

"Careful," Noah warned me. He pointed at the creeping vine near the book, but now I knew better.

I realized that the book seemed to somehow recognize poison ivy too.

I opened the cover.

"Noah! Look!" I pointed, and the two of us watched as the Scaremaster had something to say:

You shouldn't have thrown me away like garbage. Wait till you see what I have planned next! This will be the best summer ever... for me.

Chapter Seven

"It's not really a story, is it?" Noah said as we sat on that rock. "I mean it started out with 'Once upon a time,' but then it turned into threats."

I had an answer for that. "He's writing it as he goes along," I said. "There's a basic plan, but the Scaremaster responds to what you and I do." I started to explain what I saw as clues. "At first he challenged you that he could do a better prank, right?"

"So he coordinated the food fight." Noah considered it. "I still don't get how he arranged everyone to be involved." He had to admit, "I don't think I could have caused that much chaos. It was masterful."

"You sound like you admire his skill." Sometimes Noah annoyed me.

He bit a fingernail. "Well, first, he had to get the counselors on board. That couldn't have been easy. I wonder who he talked to first: Samantha or Sydney?"

"He didn't talk to anyone because the Scaremaster is not a person!" I was talking really loud, as if that would convince him. "A real person could never have gotten the counselors to make such a mess." I added to my clues: "And don't forget that later that night, he had the counselors organizing raids!"

"Strange but true," Noah said. "Maybe this book has some kind of mind-control powers?"

"I think it's bigger than just mind control. I don't know what the limits are to the Scaremaster's power." After a full body shiver, I went to my next clue: "We told the Scaremaster what he was doing wasn't fun."

"Or funny," Noah added. "I wrote that in really big letters."

"And he replied that it wasn't going to be any fun anymore." I looked at Noah.

"I see your point. He warned us." Noah continued to review everything that had happened since we'd found the book. "Making everyone do work at camp isn't funny—it's terrible." He sat for a long moment, then said, "You're convincing me."

"The campers are frightened." I turned on the rock to face him. "The Scaremaster is on track for whatever big plans he told us about the first time we read a story." I reminded him what the original Scaremaster's tale said. "And it's *done* tonight—Sunday."

"At sunset," Noah remembered. "By Monday morning, he said that everyone will know what he's done."

"Now you see why I think the Scaremaster is not like you or me. We can't just try to find him and make him stop." I liked it better when we were arguing if the Scaremaster was a he or a she. Again, I had to say, "It's not a person."

It didn't look like Noah was totally sold on my theory, but he said, "So let's stop...it."

"I wish I knew how," I said.

Noah held the book behind his back, as if it might be able to hear as well as write, and whispered to me, "You think that whatever appears in that book comes true."

"Yes," I said.

"You also think that the Scaremaster responds to what we do," Noah said.

"Yes."

"Then we need to change the story." Noah stood up from the rock. "And make a different ending."

"How? It's one thing to figure out that the Scaremaster is running camp, but another to actually stop him. We'd need to find out *what* he's doing."

"And *why*..." Noah finished my thought and added, "I mean, why wouldn't he just write a story called 'The Scaremaster Gets Everything He Wants' and be done with all this?"

"I think it's because this way is more fun for him," I suggested, but I wasn't sure.

There was a lot we needed to discover.

I looked up toward the morning sun and frowned. "We only have until sunset."

I wasn't certain we could solve this mystery in time. Maybe the Scaremaster was right. Maybe it was simply too late.

Chapter Eight

We went back to camp with a plan. It wasn't a great plan, but it was something.

I was going to the SRC to see what the movie was all about, while Noah went to the infirmary. Maybe whatever we saw would give us some kind of indication what to do next. And how to end it.

I had to find a way to watch the movie without anyone watching me. Sneak in. Sneak out. If a counselor saw me, I might never be able to get back to Noah.

Noah had a similar issue. Kids in the infirmary didn't seem to come back again. He needed to find out why and not let it happen to him.

After we investigated, we'd meet up at the flagpole to report our findings and plan the next step. It wasn't a hidden spot, but since the day began, we hadn't seen anyone else wandering around outside, so it seemed safe enough.

"Twenty minutes," Noah told me, though neither of us had a watch.

"Okay," I agreed. I'd figure out when the time was up.

"Starting now," Noah said, and we both hurried away.

The next thing I knew, Noah was in the SRC, sitting next to me on the floor at the far back, shaking my shoulders and forcing me to look into his eyes.

"We have to get you out of here," Noah said, tipping his head back over his shoulder to three kids. There was Becky, the one from my cabin who'd been forcibly removed from the food fight. That nerdy third grader also from the dining hall rebellion. And an older boy I'd never seen before. Maybe he was a CIT. They were all moving very slowly, hidden in shadows.

"Huh?" My head was thick. I couldn't think clearly, and my tongue was sort of numb. "I'll thay here. I wike the movie," I managed to say. My eyes wanted to watch the film. They were being pulled back to the screen like it was a magnet.

Noah grabbed the sides of my face and wouldn't let me look. He whispered, "Kaitlin, do you remember that you were supposed to meet me at the flagpole?"

I nodded. "Twenty minutes." I mumbled. Oh, the movie…I couldn't even remember what it was about, but I wanted to see it. So badly. I tried to pull my head back, but Noah wouldn't let go. He was holding on to my ears.

I realized we were in the storage closet. With that came a flash of memory. I had snuck in through the storage closet window (I was getting good at slipping through windows) and sat on the floor in a place where I could see the screen, but no one could see me because I was partially blocked by the door. I'd immediately noticed that no one was looking at me anyway. They were all fixated on the movie.

I did notice that there were no counselors or staff in the SRC. It was all campers, and no one was moving. They were watching the movie.

Oh...the movie...I wanted to see more.

"Let me watch," I told Noah, struggling to turn away from him. "Just a wittle more." My tongue was so, so tired.

"You've been here two hours!" Noah said.

That got my attention. "Huh?"

"Two hours." He looked at his "team," and they all nodded.

"There's no way..." I said, "way" sounding like "sway."

"Let's get out of here," Noah told me. "We have to find a place to talk."

They made me go first out the window because Noah was afraid if I didn't go first, I wouldn't go at all.

Noah followed me, and Becky followed him. Ethan, the third grader, was next. When we turned back for the kid I didn't know, he wasn't there.

"Man down!" Becky exclaimed but not very loud. She quickly consulted the others. "No man left behind," Becky insisted. They decided to take a vote on what to do.

It was two to one, Ethan and Noah against Becky.

That settled it. They wouldn't go back for him. I was so out of it and loopy, I didn't get a vote. Becky protested. "But—"

Noah said, "It's too dangerous."

I was born in China, and I'd heard that Becky's family was from China too. But other than that, we didn't seem to have very much in common. We'd barely spoken to each other since the first day of camp. Now we were thrust together in a nightmare. "Pl-ea-se, Becky." I tipped my head back toward the SRC.

"We'll save him later," Becky assured me. "We will save them all."

We hurried to my cabin. Everyone agreed that, from what they'd seen, the cabins were the safest place to be at camp. The whole area was vacant and quiet.

Once inside, Noah asked if I had black clothing. I didn't, but since no one was around to ask, we "borrowed" items from my cabin mates and counselors.

Becky had long hair, longer than mine, that

she wore in a braid down her back. She tucked it up under a black cap. She put on black pants and a black shirt. Ethan, who was a skinny redhead with freckles, found a shirt that matched hers. Noah was a little reluctant to wear Josie's black pajama pants with Samantha's shirt, but Becky convinced him we all had to match.

In pitch dark, it would be hard to tell us apart. Funny thing was, it wasn't even noon yet.

Becky told me, "Our small but mighty squad is prepared to fight all night long. We are Camp Redwood Vines' only hope." She put her hands on her hips and thrust out her chest. It was clear that Becky was the toughest one of our group.

I looked hard at us all. We were dressed for a bank robbery. As Becky helped tuck my hair under a cap, my head still felt like I'd ridden one too many roller coasters. "Thanks," I said, with the words coming out and sounding like "Flank-tzzz." I hoped my tongue would go back to normal soon.

Becky smeared Samantha's black eye liner under my eyes, like charcoal, then did the others.

"We are commandos," Becky announced. "And now we roll."

Before we left the cabin, I needed to ask a burning question. "What. Happened. To. Me?" I pronounced each word slowly. I was pretty convinced I'd been hypnotized by the movie. My tongue was gradually working better, and I managed to ask, "What's going on in the SRC?"

"Our theory is reprogramming," Noah told me. "It's a long movie that has some kind of power to erase the brain and reset it. Kids are absorbing what they need to know for the work they are going to do."

"As far as we can tell, the camp is turning into a factory," Becky said, tugging her cap more firmly onto her head and scowling into a mirror hanging by Sydney's bed.

"What kind of factory?" I asked, leaning forward expectantly.

Becky and Ethan exchanged glances. Ethan didn't say anything.

"We don't know," Becky admitted.

"We hoped you found out while you were in *there*," Noah told me.

"I don't remember anything after sneaking in the window, until you rescued me," I said, then realized, "You've rescued me a lot, Noah. First the plants, now the hypnotic movie." From the bottom of my heart I said, "Thanks."

"It's cool." Noah slapped me on the back, then said, "We need to get back to the infirmary."

I didn't understand. "What's there?"

"The book," Noah told me with a long sigh. "I got caught and hid it."

It was clear that a lot had happened while I was in the movie. "Catch me up, please," I begged.

"I'm going to say this one time, and only one time, so listen good: You were right, Kaitlin," Noah said. "The Scaremaster isn't a person, and he has this place under his not-human thumb."

I had a little surge of pride. Noah came around. I knew he would. Then again, it might have been the head fuzz, but I wasn't entirely sure what he meant. I needed more info before I celebrated this small victory.

Noah explained, "The counselors are in a trance. The campers are getting put in trances too."

I had a thought. "Noah, remember in the food fight, when you saw the counselors in the staff lounge watching a movie? What if it was the same movie the campers are seeing now? Maybe the Scaremaster was taking over their brains too." That would explain how so much time had passed while I was in the SRC, and why I'd never felt hungry. No one in the SRC had eaten in a long time. Their brains were under the Scaremaster's control, and if he didn't let them feel hungry, they didn't. That meant the counselors weren't eating either. But then I had another thought.

"That can't be right," I backtracked. "The counselors were in the dining hall at the food fight." The excitement I'd felt a second earlier disappeared. "They couldn't be in the staff lounge and the dining hall at the same time."

Noah stepped back and sat down on a lower bunk. "I'll tell you what happened in the infirmary. Maybe that will link the clues." He took a breath and began, "Jayesh and Samantha were the ones that caught me outside. They were guarding the building."

"They're so mean," Becky said. "When me and Ethan were sent there, they would come in and yell that if we were too sick to play along with the mischievous pranks, then we had to lie in bed."

She added, "They were nothing like they were at the beginning of camp." Becky imitated Samantha. She wagged a finger and paced the floor. " 'You will not leave the bed. Do not get up. There will be no activities. When you feel better, the only thing you'll be allowed to do is see a movie.' "

Noah went on. "Just after I got there, Jayesh and Samantha started bragging about the factory and how great it was going to be. I think they wanted to scare us. Kids in the movie would go to work. Kids in the infirmary—well, they were vague about what would happen to us. They let our imaginations think the worst."

"A few kids immediately claimed to feel better. I'm sure they thought their chances of survival were better in the movie than in the infirmary," Becky told me.

"The counselors went to take them to the SRC, and that was when the four of us made our escape." Hearing Noah talk about the *four* of them reminded us of the poor guy we'd left in the SRC.

Ethan was quiet, and Becky frowned.

"So, you're telling me that everyone at camp will be working for the Scaremaster's factory?" I asked, giving Noah a small shove to move over so I could sit next to him on the bed. "That means we know *what* he's planning," I said.

"And that now leaves *why* is he doing this?" Noah sat up.

"Let's go get the journal," I said. "We have to figure out a way to trick the Scaremaster into revealing the next chapter in his story."

Chapter Nine

I was getting hungry. It was past noon. The campers were still in the SRC. The big bell that called the camp for meals hadn't rung.

"No food?" I asked Ethan and Becky. The four of us were a team now.

Ethan's stomach rumbled.

"We never had breakfast," Becky reminded us.

Noah led us on a quick stop at his cabin on the way to the infirmary. At the bottom of his trunk, way below where he'd found the Scaremaster's journal, he had a tin box filled with snacks.

"You aren't supposed to have that," I said, eyeing the candy, nuts, granola bars, and beef jerky. "No outside food in the cabins."

"Feel free to tell Director Dave," he said to me with a challenging smirk.

We'd been through a lot together since the

boating prank and had so much more to do before the day was over. "I'll tell him"—I tore the wrapper off a chocolate bar and downed it in a few bites—"tomorrow." I added, "Unless we eat all the evidence."

Noah laughed.

The four of us had a fast picnic, stuffing our pockets with some reserve snacks in case dinner was also not happening at camp.

We snuck by the SRC, and it was still quiet inside, except for the faint music coming from the film.

"We should stop and see how the film's going," I suggested, feeling the pull of the movie. "If we watch, we might understand what he's making."

"Close ranks," Becky said. Ethan grabbed one of my arms and Becky the other. They dragged me away.

"I don't understand why I want to see that movie so much," I told them as we hid behind some large trees in back of the infirmary. "I don't even know what it's about."

I shook off the feeling that I wanted to go back to the SRC and stepped out from behind the tree.

I immediately fell to my hands and knees in the dirt. Noah and the others dropped down next to me.

"Just like real commandos," Becky whispered.

I whispered back, "That was close."

Jayesh and Samantha were walking past the infirmary. I overheard Jayesh tell Samantha, "We need to get back to the meeting." They turned down a small path toward the boat dock.

We saw them disappear into the distance, which is why it was really confusing an instant later when voices came from inside the infirmary. The voices were loud, but that wasn't the confusing part.

"Someone just discovered we're AWOL," Becky told us.

Just then, the front door crashed open, and Sydney came out first, followed by...

"Is that Jayesh?" I squinted.

"No way..." Noah said, his voice trailing off.

"Yes, it is. That's him," Ethan said, speaking for the first time since my rescue. "I'd know him anywhere. He's the nature specialist." He pushed up his glasses. "I like nature. Especially rocks." He reached into his pants' pocket and pulled out a handful of different colored rocks. "I collect them."

"I'll introduce you to my parents," Noah said under his breath, more a mutter than an invitation.

Ethan's eyes lit up. "Really? Thanks. I follow their blog."

Noah rolled his eyes. "I didn't know you liked their work. Most people get all weird around me when they find out about my parents, as if they are big celebrities."

I didn't want to say anything, but hadn't he noticed that Ethan hadn't spoken a word till this moment?

Then Noah noticed. "Wait," he said with a moan. "Oh no! You're one of those, aren't you?"

"Those?" I asked.

"My parents have superfans." Noah looked to Ethan, who slowly nodded. "They call themselves hugnuts."

"I'm a tree-hugging hugnut." Ethan looked at Noah. "I don't know what to say when I'm around you," he admitted. "When I first heard you were here, I was excited. Your parents are awesome cool." His face was happy, then changed. "I admired you because you get to be with them every day—you're so lucky!" He paused, lowered his voice, and added, "Then I was in the boat that sank."

"Funny prank, right?" Noah glared at me, waiting for Ethan's answer.

"No," Ethan said. "Wet and cold." He added,

"I lost three rocks in the lake." Ethan frowned. "They were my favorites. Two sedimentary and one metamorphic."

"Noah, you owe Ethan three extra-cool rocks," I said.

"But I saved the kid from the infirmary!" Noah protested.

"Uh," Becky interrupted. "There's some question about who saved who in the infirmary...."

Noah waved her off.

"Three rocks, Noah." I wasn't going to let this injustice pass. "And you should offer him a video chat with your parents."

Becky was on my side, so Noah caved.

"Sure. Whatever. But first we need to get out of this mess," Noah said, focusing us back on task. "Okay, so we just saw Jayesh pass by *and* come out of the infirmary. What does that mean?"

"They circled back?" I suggested. A possessed journal was enough of a logical leap for me. I couldn't wrap my head around another supernatural occurrence. "How about this: Jayesh is a twin, and you didn't know it, Noah."

"Can't be." Noah shook his head.

"Come on. No more chatter." Becky leapt to her feet and was moving fast toward the infirmary door. "Operation Book Back is a go!"

Sydney and the second Jayesh were gone. They'd probably gone to the director's office to report that campers were missing.

"We don't have long," Noah said, bringing up the rear as we entered the infirmary building. "Let's get the book and get away."

The infirmary was empty, and the book was right where Noah had left it. I was so relieved. Operation Book Back was a huge success. Until the infirmary door opened.

We each dove beneath a cot. I was getting tired of hiding. Since we'd found the book, this was the third time, or the fourth time, we'd crashed to the ground. My knees were starting to hurt.

I peeked out from under the bed to see that the two who entered were Sydney and Jayesh. Then again, Samantha and Sydney looked a lot alike, and from this angle, I couldn't be sure which twin had arrived. And if Noah was wrong and

Jayesh also had a twin brother, it could have been: Samantha and Jayesh 2. Or Sydney and Jayesh 2. Or Samantha and the original Jayesh.

They came in and Samantha/Sydney sat down on the bed above me. The springs creaked as the bed sagged closer to the floor.

Jayesh/Jayesh 2 sat over Noah.

That way they were facing each other, on the two beds farthest from the door, and with the door to the infirmary still open, Becky and Ethan could easily slip outside. Only thing stopping them was a good distraction.

Noah signaled Becky. She gave him a thumbs-up as he slid the journal across the floor, and she snagged it. Just in case anything happened, she'd run away as fast as she could with the book.

Now for the distraction. But what?

I considered coughing. I could get caught and taken back to the movie. That wouldn't be so bad. No, no. It was a terrible thought, and I pushed it aside immediately. No Scaremaster brainwashing movies. And yet, if I got caught, the others could escape.

I thought of other escape plans until my brain ached, but I couldn't come up with another idea.

I was going to have to give myself away for the sake of the others. Determined to be the sacrifice, I scooted forward slightly, thinking I'd just pop up and start screaming like my pants were on fire, when, suddenly, a rock clinked against the windowpane.

I turned to see that Ethan was gone! That kid was really quiet and proved it by being the first to escape. Now he was making a distraction for the rest of us.

Samantha/Sydney got up and went to the window to look out. She pulled back the black paper and said, "Someone's out there."

"One of the inmates?" Jayesh/Jayesh 2 asked.

I saw Noah and Becky exchange glances at the word "inmates," as if being in the infirmary was meant to be some kind of jail. I wondered if, by morning, Spike was going to be running the infirmary instead of the kitchen.

A second rock hit the window and Jayesh/Jayesh 2 went over to investigate with Samantha/Sydney. They looked outside.

Becky took advantage of the situation. She held the Scaremaster's book close to her chest and quick, like a ninja, slipped out the door. The door closed behind her. At first I was flipping out because she'd shut us inside! But then I realized that by slamming the door, Becky drew the counselors' attention. The two of them rushed outside to find out who had thrown the rock and if it was the same person who had slammed the door.

As they rounded the back of the building, Noah and I hurried out the front. Becky and Ethan were gone, but Becky had left us a clue to where they went. One of Noah's candy wrappers was on the ground. It would have looked like trash to the counselors, but it was a signal to us!

Noah and I didn't stop running until we were in his cabin. Becky and Ethan were there waiting. We waited in silence a few moments to make sure we hadn't been followed. Then, when the coast felt clear, sat in a small circle in the middle of the wooden floor.

Noah took the journal from Becky and opened it to the first page.

The Scaremaster had written a new story. And it was chilling.

Once upon a time, there was a boy named Noah and a girl

named Kaitlin. They had two
friends, Becky and Ethan.

"How does it know that?" Ethan asked, even though Noah had already explained.

"It's possessed," I said. It was getting easier to admit that the rules of the universe no longer applied to our situation.

Noah went on reading:

These naive children are about
to learn a very big lesson:

The general issues commands.

The captains obey the general
and lead the soldiers.

The soldiers make books for
the captains.

The captains give the books to
the general.

Every day the general recruits
new captains and new soldiers.

These soldiers will make
more books.

The prisoners do not know what
is happening.

More and more books will be
made every day.

And when the books are done,
the general will have the largest
army in the world.

As for Noah, Kaitlin, Becky,
and Ethan, their fate is grim.
They are the enemies. When
the sun sets, all enemies will
be doomed.

"The Scaremaster tells the worst stories," Noah said, putting down the book. "This one is like bad, confusing poetry."

Becky asked if she could see the book. "No, it's still a story," she said. "A very scary short story."

I had the vibe the Scaremaster was speaking in a language Becky understood. "Are your parents in the military?" I asked.

"Isn't it obvious?" Noah said. With a glance at Becky, he explained, "No offense, but you talk like a soldier."

She knit her eyebrows, and a shadow fell over her face. "My dad and mom met when he was stationed at a base near her university in China. When they moved to the States, we thought he'd have an office job and stay around, but now Dad has been deployed for nearly two years. Every time he's supposed to return, he gets a new assignment."

I knew some military families in my neighborhood. It was really hard for kids to only see their mom or dad once in a while on a computer screen. As much as I complained about my parents' hovering, I was certain Becky would have traded places with me in a heartbeat.

Ethan pointed at the journal and asked her, "Can you tell us what the story means?"

Becky read it out loud again. Then she said, "This is about the chain of command—my parents talk about that all the time. It's how a military gets its orders: The soldiers listen to the captains. The captains have to report back to the generals. It seems to me that the Scaremaster is setting himself up as the ultimate general." Becky considered what she was saying. "But this is all wrong," she told us. "As a soldier, my dad is helping to make the world a better place. I don't get all this doomed stuff." She added, "There are also a lot of other ranks like majors, lieutenants, corporals...I could go on all day. Plus, there are ranks within the ranks. You'd think the Scaremaster would know all that!"

"It's a metaphor," I replied. I might not be the same kind of writer as the Scaremaster, but still, an investigative journalist is also a writer. "I think he's saying that whatever he's up to will be over at sundown, like he warned us. And..." I had another thought. "'Doomed' might mean that there will be no more fun, not just at this camp, but all the camps around the lake." It might be bigger. "Or in the whole world."

"How could the Scaremaster get to all camps, everywhere?" Becky asked, raising the book and rotating it in her hands. "He's only telling stories in this one journal."

"He's making more books." That was Ethan. He shivered the instant the words were out. And in that moment, the Scaremaster's entire plan became clear to me. By the look in Noah and Becky's eyes, they got it too.

"The campers are going to build a factory," I said. "They are clearing the cemetery and laying out wood for construction. Other supplies, probably leather and pages, were taken to the maintenance shed."

"They will probably start with a few books made in the SRC, then move to the factory once it's done!" Becky took off her knit cap and rubbed it across her forehead. "Oh man, this is bad."

"The counselors, like the story's captains, will be overseeing operations." Noah took off his hat as well. We were quickly losing our commando look.

I was not going to give up. I tugged my cap even more firmly onto my head and said, "The

Scaremaster's going to send journals to all the summer camps and try to create more and more Scaremaster minions making journals. Soon he'll have enough leather journals to give to kids everywhere. Whatever he writes in those stories comes true." I gave my hat another tug. "If he succeeds, the Scaremaster will take over the world with his own scary tales!"

"Our mission is clear," Becky said, standing with hands on her hips. "We have to stop the Scaremaster." She and Noah put their caps back on. Ethan made sure his was tight. We were ready.

Noah took the book and wrote to the Scaremaster:

I have some questions.

The Scaremaster immediately wrote back in his messy, scratchy scrawl:

The time for answers is over.

Just one question?

No.

I was going to ask anyway. I took the pencil:

What do you want?

The end.

After that, no matter what else I wrote, the Scaremaster didn't reply. He wasn't going to answer anything, but we'd figured out most of what we needed to know.

We knew *who* he was: the Scaremaster, a scary storyteller who could control events through his journal.

We knew *what* he wanted: a factory to make journals.

And now we knew *why*.

Noah summed it up: "With Scaremaster journals throughout the world, the Scaremaster can be in many places at once. He can write his stories, and anyone who reads them would be manipulated by him to do whatever he wants. It's like he's cloning his evil self...."

"Cloning...right," I echoed.

My investigator brain started to review what

we knew: The Scaremaster was manipulating everything.

The campers were being reprogrammed. But how were the counselors involved?

They weren't in the SRC watching the movie. During the food fight, Noah had seen counselors watching a different video in the staff lounge, and I'd seen others walking around camp. Sometimes we ran into the same counselors twice.

"Noah, you're a genius!" I leapt across our little circle and gave him a hug. "Guys! The counselors are being cloned!"

Chapter Ten

Noah struggled to break free. "You're suffocating me," he complained.

I was hugging him really hard, but he deserved the biggest, best hug ever.

Letting go, I rocked back on my heels and sat with folded legs. "The counselors are in a comatose trance. The movie they're watching has trapped them. The clone counselors are taking over." This was big. Bigger than I ever imagined. "What are we going to do?"

"Like Noah said before—we have to change the Scaremaster's story's ending," Ethan said. Now that we'd bonded over a common goal, Ethan was talking more.

"We can't change the story," Becky told him. "The battle's begun. It's the four of us versus an army of clones. We must fight."

"I have an idea." Noah dragged his trunk out

again. "The Scaremaster isn't the only one with a journal."

"Noah Silvetti's Big Book o' Pranks?" I asked, curiosity rising.

"Exactly," Noah said, turning through the pages of his spiral notebook. I wasn't surprised to find that it that really did have a cover made of flower seeds. "We need to trap the counselor clones and get them out of the way before we free the real counselors." He began reading off prank ideas from his book. "Put a bed on the roof? That would be annoying, but I doubt we can catch them that way. Duct tape them together?" Neither of those ideas were what we needed.

He read on, "Smear Vaseline on the door-knobs. Play trumpet at three a.m." He shook his head. "These are basic pranks, not a way to trap a whole group of evil counselor clones. I need bigger ideas—like maybe we can chase them into a pit?" Noah rejected that. He turned a few more pages. "Trap them in a net?" He rejected that too.

"Anything else in there?" Becky asked, seeing that he was getting toward the end of the notebook.

"Six pages of things you can do with shaving cream," Noah said, wrinkling his eyebrows.

I could feel time slipping past. The longer we took to come up with something, the closer the campers were to becoming evil minions. The movie wouldn't go on forever. In fact, I was suddenly worried about how much time there was left. Outside, the sunlight was already getting dimmer.

"Pick one, Noah," I said in a frustrated rush of words. "We gotta get going." Then it came to me. I didn't even say anything. I just smiled big, with all my teeth showing.

"You look like you know how to trap the clones," Ethan said.

"We aren't going to trap them at all," I said. Then seeing everyone staring at me, I pointed outside where the sun was already getting lower on the horizon. "We're running out of time." I opened the door and checked for any movement outside. After I felt like the coast was clear, I said, "We have to hurry."

They trusted me enough to follow.

We headed out, but then I stopped so fast Becky bumped into me. I looked past her to Noah and asked, "Do you have any plastic gloves?"

"Of course I do. My parents insisted I bring them. They wouldn't let me come here without a promise to bring back multiple different plant spec-imens," Noah said, hurrying back to his trunk. "Finally, something I packed for the summer will be useful!"

This was the most important investigation of my life.

First, we needed confirmation that what we'd figured out together was true.

We went by the SRC and checked that the campers were still watching the movie. That was good—in a bad way. They shouldn't be stuck like that, but it was good that they weren't moving, so we knew where to find them. And I was relieved to discover that I didn't feel pulled to go watch the movie with them this time.

Then we went to the staff lounge, the last place Noah had seen our normal counselors. They were there, just like he'd described. Through a small slit in a blackened window, we could see the entire camp staff sitting on couches, pillows or on the floor, entranced by a movie. Again good, but bad.

I was seriously worried about running into the

counselor clones, but we didn't. That was also good. Though I did wonder where they were, I was sure the Scaremaster needed them for when the movie ended. I crossed my fingers and hoped my plan would succeed before that happened.

We hurried to the meadow beyond the camp property. Noah had the Scaremaster's journal. I asked him for it. We sat on the same flat rock where we'd spoken to the Scaremaster...that same morning. Wow. So much had happened since we'd retrieved the book from the hollowed-out tree nearby.

"Noah, we are going to need some of that poison ivy," I said, remembering how the book seemed to recoil from it earlier.

"Do you know how to pick it?" Noah asked Ethan. "You have to be careful."

"I learned all about nature's natural defenses from Nina and John Silvetti's first book, *Back to the Basics*," Ethan said, blushing as he looked at Noah.

"Ugh. I'd nearly forgotten...." Noah looked at

me and pointed his thumb at Ethan. "He's a very happy hugnut."

"Don't forget, you owe him a meet-up," I said with a smile.

Noah rolled his eyes. "My parents will love him."

Ethan's obsession with nature turned out to be helpful, especially when combined with Noah's vast knowledge. Wearing the gloves he'd brought, Noah collected the poison ivy leaves while Ethan collected something he called *"Helenium autumnale."*

"What's that?" Becky asked.

Ethan translated to non-sciencespeak: "Sneezeweed." And explained, "In the olden days, some people thought that sneezing would get rid of bad spirits that had invaded the body. Doctors would create a powder from sneezeweed as a way to sneeze out the evil."

"Yes! That sounds perfect," I said.

I had this idea to change the story, and we needed to do it from inside the story itself. I had one chance to get it right. If this didn't work, the Scaremaster would win, and by morning, we'd all be his servants.

I explained my plan. "Remember how you all turned my head away from the screen to get me out of the reprogramming movie? If I couldn't see the movie, I wasn't trapped by it anymore."

"I see what you are saying," Becky said. "But couldn't the same result be achieved by a reconnaissance operation to cut electricity?" It was a good point.

"I don't know where the power supply is, do you? And we can't get close enough to the projector to unplug it—unless we want to be zombified."

Becky agreed. This was our only chance.

I opened the journal to the Scaremaster's story.

"When Noah and I were here last, I noticed that the book seemed to pull away from poison ivy, as if it was scared. I'm hoping I found a weakness. So let's try this: Put on gloves, then everywhere you see the word 'soldier,'" I told Noah, "rub sneezeweed on the words."

"Are the soldiers the campers?" he asked me.

"If I'm right, then yes," I said, fingers crossed that I had this figured out.

"Ethan, where it says 'prisoner,' that stands for our real counselors. Smear the page with poison ivy."

I watched them work their gloved hands down the page.

These naive children are about
to learn a very big lesson:

The general issues commands.

The captains obey the general
and lead the **soldiers**.

The **soldiers** make books for the
captains.

The captains give the books to
the general.

Every day the general recruits
new captains and new **soldiers**.

These **soldiers** will make
more books.

*The **prisoners** do not know what is happening.*

More and more books will be made every day.

And when the books are done, the general will have the largest army in the world.

As for Noah, Kaitlin, Becky, and Ethan, their fate is grim. They are the enemies. When the sun sets, all enemies will be doomed.

"What about the 'captains'?" Becky asked me. "I'm pretty sure those refer to the counselor clones. How are we going to stop them?"

I didn't have an answer for that—yet. I didn't know where to find the counselor clones, but if this worked, we had a room of real counselors too itchy to watch a movie, and campers who couldn't see the screen because they were busy sneezing.

And that meant, if I was right, everyone would be normal again. And if we could convince them the clones were evil, we'd have an army of our own! A Redwood Vines army that could defeat the Scaremaster and his wicked clones.

It was time to gather our troops.

Chapter Eleven

The sun slid down behind the horizon, and darkness settled at camp.

At Becky's call—"Company march!"—we *ran*. Straight through the woods, back to the path, and into the center of camp.

As we went, my biggest worry was that we had no Plan B.

The Scaremaster could still win. We'd be captured and reprogrammed from campers into Scaremaster bookmakers. My parents would worry when they didn't get my daily letter, but I bet the Scaremaster had a plan for that too. Fake letters, maybe.

At the end of the summer, he'd probably let us go because his journals would be everywhere, all over the world, and he could write stories whenever he wanted. It was going to be a total Scaremaster takeover! This was scarier than any scary movie I'd ever seen. But worse, because it was really happening.

My heart was pounding in my head as we reached camp. I kept my fingers crossed and repeated, "Let it work…." over and over so many times that anyone listening would have thought I was stuck in a loop.

And then, as we rounded the flagpole, heading into the center of camp, I knew I didn't have to worry. My heart settled, and an excitement built as we rushed to the SRC. First I heard the sneezing. It was like someone released cats into a room of kids with allergies. *Achoos* echoed from inside the building.

Sneezing campers began streaming out of the building, not in an orderly flow, but looking like a concert just ended. Kids rushed through the main door, all jumbled up in a massive crowd.

Noah thought it was hysterical, the way everyone was sneezing and bumping into each other as they walked. Plus, they were talking as if bricks were tied to their tongues.

"Wood work," he said to me, imitating the others. Punctuating it with a fake "Achoo."

"Thanks," I replied, knowing he was goofing around. "It *was* good work!"

Noah raised the Scaremaster's journal and stopped pretending he had a thick head and a heavy tongue. "I know he intended this to be terrifying, as he built an army of clones, but instead, the Scaremaster created human bumper cars." At that, two girls from my cabin knocked into each other on unsteady feet. They both fell gently to the ground in a tangled heap of arms and legs. "I wish I'd been the one to think of smearing sneezeweed in the book. This is the funniest prank, and it wasn't even mine." Noah bowed to me. "You really are royalty, Your Highness. From now on, you are officially the queen of pranks."

"It wasn't meant to be a prank," I told him.

"Ah, but it still counts." Noah laughed as the CIT we'd left behind bumped into a tree. Leaves rained down on his head.

"Luckily, the effects from the movie wear off fast," I said. "Well, pretty fast," I corrected myself, remembering how some symptoms lingered. I honestly had no idea how long the sneezing would go on.

"I'll enjoy it while it lasts," Noah said. Already some kids were starting to come out of the trance.

Knowing that there'd be a few campers who,

like me, were in it so deep that they'd try to go back inside for the end of the film, Becky and Ethan patrolled the SRC and the area outside, while Noah and I pulled every electrical cord we could find. Just for added safety.

"Operation Save Camp Clone, Phase One is a success," Becky told Noah and me. "Commence Phase Two."

It was time to check out what had happened with our counselors.

Noah and I dashed from the SRC to the staff lounge. The counselors weren't outside. I peeked through the window, anxious about what I'd find. The counselors were inside, scratching their own backs or other counselors' backs. On the other side of the room, I could clearly see Director Dave rubbing his arms.

"We did it!" I told Noah. "No one is watching TV. They're all too busy scratching! That means, no one's in a trance anymore."

We gave each other a fist bump, then went to open the door.

"How long will the itching last?" I figured Noah would know. When he didn't answer me right away, I turned to see that he wasn't facing me—he was staring out at the mob that was headed our way.

It was the clones! The first ones I saw were the fake Samantha and Sydney, followed by evil imitations of Jayesh and Michael—they all had the same blank look on their faces. They were staring straight ahead, looking at us, but not really seeing us. It was like whatever went into their brains didn't compute. I thought about the times the twins laughed and the chaos they made in the dining hall. The clones were definitely being controlled by the Scaremaster.

The clone versions of our counselors streamed toward us from the direction of the art shed, followed by the administrators, the nurse, and that cute couple who did maintenance. Only they weren't so cute now. They were super scary with their messy hair and blank expressions.

But now the Scaremaster's story had been changed. So the Scaremaster responded.

Director Dave pushed his way through the

others to lead the pack. He had a similar vacant expression, but there I could sense the anger behind those dark, empty eyes.

"The Scaremaster must be leading them," I said. "And they're after us!"

The cloned counselors fanned out to surround us. I looked left and right; there was no escape. And if we went into the lounge, we'd be trapped inside. There was no rear door.

"Noah!" I said. "What should we do?" The investigator in me, always looking for details, noticed that the clones' eyes weren't looking at me or Noah; instead, they were fastened on *Tales from the Scaremaster* in Noah's hands. "I think they want the book!"

Noah was frozen.

Had the Scaremaster somehow taken over Noah without a movie or TV? I didn't know what was happening, but the more I shook his shoulder, the stiffer he became. "Noah, this isn't the time for a joke!"

The counselor clones were getting closer. We'd had this plan for the campers and real counselors to be our army against the clones, but now I could see that the campers were still too zoned out and the counselors too itchy. We seriously needed a Plan B. Why didn't we have a Plan B?

"Help!" Noah shouted toward Becky and Ethan. I could see them over by the SRC, still dealing with the sneezing campers. By the time they got to us, it would be done. The Scaremaster would win. He'd have his clone army here and his soldiers making books for other camps! I had to stop him, but how?

I looked at Noah, the fear on his face was real as he stared out at the clones, holding the book tight against his chest. "What do we do, Kaitlin?" he asked. Noah, it seemed, was finally out of ideas.

Noah had saved me so many times during the weekend; it was my turn. Without really thinking about what I was doing, I grabbed the Scaremaster's book out of his hands.

If the clones wanted the journal, then let them come after me to get it!

Feeling pretty confident that the clones would leave Noah and follow me, I held the book tight to my chest and took off. Becky would have been proud as I ran straight into the enemy's front line.

I ducked and dodged anyone who tried to slow me down.

I imagined that the hands that grabbed for the book were tennis balls, and with the book as my racquet, I swung at them, knocking them away.

As I expected, the mob came after me. This was all about the Scaremaster. He needed the clones to get the book and put his story back on track.

I ran, full speed, back to the clearing. I felt sure the Scaremaster was now regretting writing such slow clones. Too bad for him. This was *my* story now.

I got to the clearing before the others and found the poison berries that Noah had pointed out to me. That guy really knew his plants!

As I opened the book, I could see the clones getting near. I had a moment of doubt over whether I could do this in time. Could I save the camp and get rid of the clones forever? All my fears faded away when I heard the voices of my platoon. It seemed that Becky, Ethan, and Noah had arrived. They'd come to help! I was happy to have them there.

Ethan tossed a clean glove to me and called out, "Good choice: *Actaea pachypoda*! The little white berries have a black—"

"Call them the common name, doll's eyes, you hugnut!" Then Noah shouted to me, "Queen of Pranks, prank the Scaremaster!"

The boys were interrupted by Becky: "Stand strong, soldier!"

Turned out I did have a Plan B after all. With my friends nearby, cheering me on, I smashed several of those poison berries between my gloved fingers, careful not to drip juice anywhere on the page except exactly where I wanted it.

Noah had said that the berries would bring "a fate worse than slipping on Jell-O." That's what I needed. Something way worse than death by Jell-O. Very cautiously, I smeared doll's eye juice across everywhere in the story it said: captains.

*The **captains** obey the general and lead the soldiers.*

*The soldiers make books for the **captains**.*

The **captains** give the books to
the general.

Every day the general recruits
new **captains** and new
soldiers.

I didn't really think a little berry juice would
shut down the Scaremaster's stories forever, but I
had some extra juice, so I made a quick swipe over
the word "general" in five places.

The **general** issues commands.

The captains obey the **general**
and lead the soldiers.

The captains give the books to
the **general**.

Every day the **general** recruits
new captains and new soldiers.

And when the books are done,
*the **general** will have the largest*
army in the world.

The effect on the clones was immediate. They disappeared. Just like that. One minute they were after me, and the next they were gone.

I checked the book. The Scaremaster's entire story had vanished! There were no more words on the page, just a few stains where I'd swiped the berry juice.

Becky, Noah, and Ethan rushed to me, and we hugged. It was the best hug ever. We were bonded together, celebrating what we'd done. When we broke apart, we danced around a little and high-fived each other, careful, of course, not to fall into any poisonous plants.

I laughed and announced, "I'm a happy hugnut now!" And we hugged a little more.

We were heroes.

The Scaremaster's story had come to an end.

Chapter Twelve

Monday morning, I met Noah outside the dining hall.

"I can't believe we have KP!" I exclaimed. "After everything we did..."

"No one remembers what happened," Noah said with a small laugh. "Crazy, right? It's like the whole weekend was a dream."

"It's not so crazy. Remember when you told me that two hours had passed in that movie? I thought it was twenty minutes." I tucked my hair under my Camp Redwood Vines hat.

Noah started to say something, but just then, Director Dave arrived. Becky and Ethan were with him.

"Seems that a weekend of KP wasn't enough," he said, his bald head glistening in the early morning sun. "I think a whole week will bring you around to shape this ship."

Becky raised her hand as if we were in school, and without being called on she said, "It's shipshape, sir. It's a naval term meaning neat and in line."

He shook his head to clear it. "Oh, right. Ship-shape." He tapped his forehead. "That's what I meant."

Noah and I locked eyes. Some people, it seemed, were still fuzzy-headed from the Scaremaster's brain takeover.

The director went on. "I don't know what you were thinking." He focused on Noah. "After everything your parents did to get you a spot here this summer..."

Whoa! In a flash I realized what the S in the SRC stood for—it was the Silvetti Recreation Center! Noah's parents had made a huge donation to get Noah into camp!

Noah saw my face light with the realization and gave me a subtle nod. I nodded back. His secret was safe with me.

Director Dave scratched at a red rash on his arm. "As if throwing itching powder in the staff lounge wasn't bad enough, you gave sneezing powder to all the campers!" Director Dave was angry. "This prank stuff is going too far, Noah.

I don't know how you convinced the others to be involved."

"He didn't have to convince us to do anything," I cut in. "We were in it together because we're his friends." I reached out and put a hand on Noah's shoulder. If he was in trouble, I was going to be in trouble with him—even if it meant that we'd both be looking for a new camp next year.

Ethan and Becky came and linked arms with me and Noah in a friendship chain.

"The platoon will not be divided," Becky said.

We all cheered.

Director Dave shook his head again. I couldn't tell if he wasn't thinking clearly or thought we'd all gone batty. "Whatever." He pointed to the kitchen door. "Spike is waiting. Get to work." He turned and walked away toward his office.

I dropped arms with my new friends and started to go into the kitchen.

"Hang on," Noah said, stopping me first, then the others. "We're already in trouble, so it won't matter if we're late." After checking that Director Dave was out of sight, he took a few steps away from the dining hall. "We have to get rid of the Scaremaster's book. I know just the place."

"The tree?" I asked. We'd get in trouble for sure, but we all knew this was more important than slicing apples or whatever Spike had planned for the morning.

"I have a better idea," Noah said. He led the way, stopping behind the dumpster, to where he'd stashed a shovel. "I borrowed it from the maintenance shed. No one even noticed I was there. The staff was busy sorting boxes of paper and leather covers."

"The Scaremaster's factory supplies," I said. It was just like we'd thought.

"They think that it was a shipping mistake." Noah chuckled. "I cannot believe no one remembers anything!"

When we got to the old cemetery, Ethan took the shovel. He surveyed the area, which had been mowed by Noah's cabin and the fourth graders to make room for the Scaremaster's factory. After performing several soil tests, he declared, "The ground is soft enough to dig a really deep hole."

"My parents are going to want to swap kids with his parents," Noah said to me and Becky. "They'll take Ethan, and I'll live wherever he's from."

"Maybe it'll all work out. You never know, Ethan's parents might have a great sense of humor," I suggested.

"You're getting good at joking around, Katy." Noah laughed, then handed me the Scaremaster's book. "I'm coming back every summer to this camp—if you are."

I tapped the logo on my Camp Redwood Vines hat and said, "I'll be here. I heard they don't like jokes over at Camp Edwards." I added with a wink, "And they have a lame recreation center."

Ethan picked the perfect spot. We all took turns shoveling. The hole had to be deep.

Becky was the strongest of us all, and gradually, we gave all our turns to her. She finished fast. I gave the book one last check to see that the pages were blank, then tossed it in. It landed at the bottom of the hole with a thud. Becky immediately began refilling the hole, humming a song I didn't recognize but assumed to be from the army.

"Do you want to join the military like your dad?" I asked, feeling like the answer was obvious.

"No," she said, surprising me. "What made you think that?"

"No reason," I quickly replied.

"I want to be a kindergarten teacher like my mom," she told me as she finished up. "I love little kids."

I never would have guessed that!

Even though the last few days had been terrible, and scary, and could have been a disaster, something good had come from the Scaremaster's story. I was glad I had gotten to know Becky and Ethan. And then there was Noah—he and I were going to be friends for life.

Ethan covered the book's burial spot with heavy stones so no one would see the fresh turned dirt and come to explore.

"It's like it never existed," Noah said with certainty. "The grass will grow back quickly. Besides, no other campers are brave enough to explore the cemetery."

"We should spread a few rumors to keep them away." I winked. "Just in case."

"So what do you want to investigate next?" Noah asked me as we all walked together to the kitchen for KP.

"I'm not sure," I said, glancing over my shoulder at the mound of dirt and rocks covering *Tales from the Scaremaster*.

"Well, I'm sure there's some mystery at camp ready for you to solve, or some big secret," he suggested. "You could start a newspaper or blog."

"Maybe," I said, not committing to anything.

In truth, there *was* one more secret at camp. A big one. But I wasn't going to investigate it. Not ever. I wasn't even going to tell anyone. Not even Noah or Becky or Ethan...

Before we buried the book, when I looked inside to check that the pages were blank—they weren't blank at all.

Inside, the Scaremaster had started a fresh story. It said:

Once upon a time, there were twin brothers....

Epilogue

"Dude!" twelve-year-old Ryan called across the crowded costume shop to his brother. "You gotta see what I found!" He grabbed things off the shelf until his arms were full. "Where are you?"

The costume shop was a small space. Tall display shelves formed mazelike tight aisles. Merchandise was so packed in it made the store feel dark and crowded. And extra awesome!

"Over here. In makeup." Tyler gave what they called the "family whistle." One sharp burst followed by three softer tweets.

Ryan listened closely to pinpoint the sound, then started to run toward his brother. His straight brown hair flopped down over one eye as he dashed through the shop.

"Excuse me." A young woman with long black hair appeared in the aisle. Ryan had been moving so fast he didn't see her until it was almost too late. He managed to stop in time, but it was a serious near miss that could have been a big crash. He fumbled the things in his hands but didn't drop them.

"No running," she said, pinning him with her bright blue eyes. Her voice wasn't raised, like when he got stopped by the principal at school; rather, it was calm and firm. "We don't act like monsters in my shop." The woman handed Ryan a plastic basket with two handles. "Put the items you wish to buy in here."

Heaving a heavy sigh, Ryan dumped everything he was carrying into the basket. "Now can I—"

She held up a hand. "Let me see what you have."

The shop owner took her time going through the items Ryan had chosen. "Dirty torn shorts, muddy ripped T-shirt, red colored contact lenses, fake peeling skin, bandages..." She neatly stacked it all in a pile, then handed the newly organized orange basket back to Ryan. "Zombie, right?"

"My brother and I are going to the school Halloween dance," Ryan told her, feeling a surge of happiness. Halloween was his favorite holiday. "We're going to have the most amazing costumes!"

"Well," she said, "you're certainly off to a good start." Her blue eyes seemed to shift to green when she told him, "You'll find your brother at the end of the next aisle to the left."

"How did you know—?" Ryan started to ask.

"Twins," she said with a small smile that twinkled in her eyes, making them seem yellow. "He looks just like you."

"Of course," Ryan said with a small nod. Being a twin was a good thing and a bad thing. It was annoying when people mixed them up. But epic when they mixed themselves up on purpose.

"Go on," the woman said, pointing the way. "I'm sure you two have a lot of planning to do." She paused, still blocking his way for a few heartbeats, then stepped aside so he could pass.

Ryan shivered. There was a spark of something in the woman's now-brown eyes that was making him nervous. She was nice, so he didn't know what was giving him the chills.

Using his "best manners," just like his parents taught him, he said, "Thank you, ma'am," and walked away. Once out of her sight, he took off running again.

"What took you so long?" Tyler asked when Ryan found him, exactly where the woman said.

He looked back the way he'd come, but she was gone.

"I found some cool stuff," Ryan told Tyler, holding out the basket.

Where Ryan moved at top speed all the time, his brother was a turtle. Tyler took his time looking through the basket before saying, "Are we going to match again this year?"

"Of course," Ryan said, bouncing on his toes. "We match every year!"

"Oh." Tyler turned his attention back to the makeup. "I was sorta thinking you could be a crawler and I'd be a boney."

Tyler had spent a lot of time on the Internet reading about zombies over the past few months. He'd been the one to find this store. They'd had to take a bus there, but the online comments said the man who owned it was an expert in monsters and would have everything they needed. The reviews must have been wrong, because it seemed that the woman Ryan had met owned the store, and neither saw any men working there.

Ryan told Tyler, "Let's both be crawlers." Those were the kind of zombies with bad injuries that made them hobble along. "We can put fake blood all over our legs."

"I really wanted to be a boney," Tyler countered. Boneys had their skin peeling off so that the bones showed through.

"Whatever," Ryan said. It didn't matter what kind of zombie they were, as long as they were the same kind. They could freak people out by appearing in two places at once! It was going to be a historic Halloween, one that people remembered forever.

"Pick the makeup," he told Tyler. "I'll wear whatever you choose."

Tyler turned back to the makeup display. "Boneys," he said, more to himself than to Ryan. "We need white and red and black...." He surveyed the selection. "Liquid latex, eye liner, green slime, and dark purple paint for bruises." All that went neatly into Ryan's basket.

Ryan tried to be patient, but it was hard. When Tyler finally finished, he snagged the basket and ran to the register.

The woman with the changing eyes rang up their items.

When they heard the price, Tyler looked to Ryan. "We don't have enough money."

Ryan fished a combination of dollar bills and coins from his pocket. "We have all this!" He dumped his stash on the counter.

"I counted it last night," Tyler said, pinching his lips together. "We are going to have to put some stuff back."

Ryan sighed as Tyler started separating the items into two piles. Most of the things Ryan had picked were ending up in the put-back pile. "Can't we keep any of it?" he moaned.

"I don't think so—" Tyler was distracted, adding totals in his head. "Makeup is the important thing. Plus, it was my idea to come here...." he reminded Ryan, as if to say that meant he got first dibs on what they bought.

"But—" Ryan started to argue when the woman at the counter cut in, saying, "I have a solution for your problem."

They looked up at her. She crooked a finger. "Follow me."

The boys glanced at each other, then took off after her. The woman led them through the store and down a hallway to the back of the storage room. In the farthest corner, there was a door. It was made of intricately carved heavy wood with a polished brass handle.

The hinges creaked as the woman stepped inside.

"This is where I keep the discount items," she told them. "Only my most special customers get to come in here."

That thought made Ryan shiver. And that was soooo cool! He loved being scared! The room was creepy. The woman was creepy. He couldn't wait to see what she had hidden back here.

The instant they stepped aside, Ryan dashed over to a shelf filled with items that had a small sign on it. "Seventy-five percent off," he exclaimed. "Check it, Ty!" They both excitedly started searching through the items. "There's everything we want!"

The woman moved to the side of the room and sat in a chair that Ryan hadn't noticed at first. This wasn't just a discount room; it was also her office. A large throne chair, carved similarly to the door, with interwoven circles and strange squiggled patterns, sat behind a clean, polished desk. The smooth surface reminded Ryan of Tyler's desk at home and was nothing like his own cluttered workspace.

Ryan and Tyler started pulling things from the discount shelf, with Tyler organizing what they wanted to buy in a pile.

"You'll find expired fake blood, opened packages of peeling skin that were returned, and damaged bone pieces," the woman explained. "I can't sell any of it in the regular store."

"This is great!" Ryan cheered. Then he turned to see there was a box on the top shelf. "What's in that?" he asked her.

"I'm glad you asked," she said with a small smile. She rose from the desk and stood on her tiptoes to bring the unmarked cardboard box down. She set the box on her desk. "You can have anything in here for free."

"Really?" Ryan asked. "All this?"

Tyler stopped searching through the discount shelf and came to look. "Free is even better than discounted," he said.

Inside the free box were torn and dirtied

costumes, similar to the ones Tyler had forced Ryan to put back. There seemed to be two of everything they needed: shorts, ripped T-shirts, colored packages of contact lenses, and long strips of loose bandages!

Ryan felt weird asking but she had said "anything" and he really wanted to take it all! "Can we—" he began.

The woman interrupted, answering even though he never finished the question. "It's yours." She then took a ledger out of her drawer and turned her attention away from them, to her work.

Underneath all the old clothing, Tyler pulled out an old book. He leaned in and whispered to Ryan, "Hey, look. Do you think she meant this too?"

The woman was listening after all. She raised her head and said, "The whole box is yours. I wouldn't have offered if I didn't mean it." She noted the book in Tyler's hand. "It's an old journal. I got it from a man who dug it up from a haunted cemetery. There's only one like it in the world." She came across the room and tapped the cover. "Draw your zombie costume designs inside."

"Let me see it." Ryan took the journal from Tyler. The book felt heavy in his hand and smelled like an odd combination of dirt and metal. He pushed back a little brass locking clasp on the cover and opened the pages. "It's damaged," he leaned over, and told Tyler. "There are these weird stains all over the first page."

"Maybe that's why she wanted to give it to us for free," Tyler said. He took the book back. "It looks like marks from berries or grass." Holding the book against his chest, Tyler said, "I like it. We should take it."

On the bus home, Ryan carried the box. Tyler held the bag of discount makeup.

They were so excited to get home and explore everything they got that the ride felt like it was taking forever. To pass the time, Ryan took the journal out of the bag. He traced his finger over a strange triangle pattern etched into the cover, beneath some long scratch marks. He opened to the second page, the clean one after the berry-marked page, then made up a title and wrote it at the top.

"What else should I write?" he asked his brother.

"I don't—" Tyler started, when suddenly, Ryan

jumped up, grabbing Tyler's hand and squeezing it hard. "No way! What the heck?"

"What is going on?" Tyler yanked back his hand.

Without another word, Ryan turned the book toward his brother.

He'd written:

AWESOME ZOMBIE COSTUME IDEAS

Under that, mysterious handwriting appeared:

Zombies, is it? Oh, the Scaremaster knows a thing or two about the undead. You shouldn't have started this story. Now I get to finish it!

Read Ryan and Tyler's story
(if you dare)

in

TALES FROM THE
SCAREMASTER™

Zombie Apocalypse!

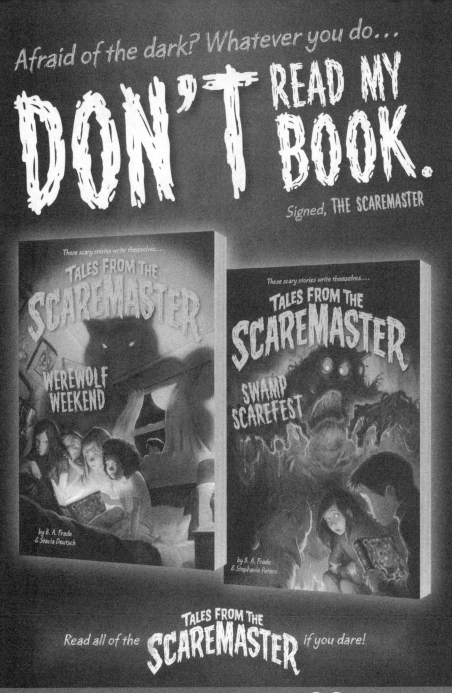

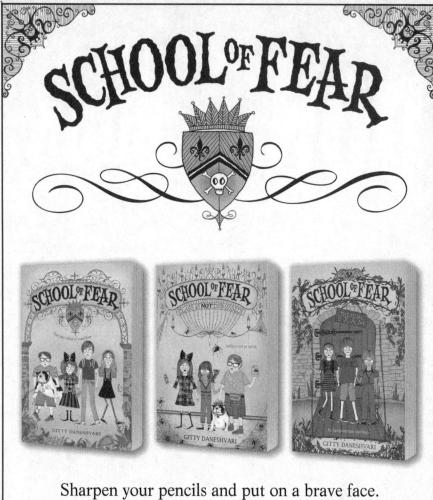